西尔科《典仪》中的离散身份问题

Diaspora Identity in Silko's *Ceremony*

卢静　著

山东大学出版社
SHANDONG UNIVERSITY PRESS
·济南·

图书在版编目(CIP)数据

西尔科《典仪》中的离散身份问题:英文/卢静著
.—济南:山东大学出版社,2021.12
ISBN 978-7-5607-7277-6

Ⅰ.①西… Ⅱ.①卢… Ⅲ.①莱斯利·马蒙·西尔科
—小说研究—英文 Ⅳ.①I712.074

中国版本图书馆 CIP 数据核字(2021)第 254491 号

责任编辑 李 璐
封面设计 王秋忆

出版发行 山东大学出版社
社 址 山东省济南市山大南路 20 号
邮政编码 250100
发行热线 (0531)88363008
经 销 新华书店
印 刷 济南新科印务有限公司
规 格 880 毫米×1230 毫米 1/32
5.625 印张 151 千字
版 次 2021 年 12 月第 1 版
印 次 2021 年 12 月第 1 次印刷
定 价 31.00 元

Foreword

Diasporic groups suffer from both geographical and psychological displacement. Neither homeland nor hostland culture is the consolation for their diaspora experiences, which eventually leads to the situation of cultural default and identity loss. So I argue for a new constitution of diaspora identity to provide diasporic groups with solutions for their sufferings.

This study focuses on the problem of diaspora and diaspora identity. For the definition of diaspora, it emphasizes the aspect of psychological displacement as a determining factor in diaspora experiences. The attitudes towards homeland and hostland culture and the mental status of displaced groups decide whether they belong to diasporas or not. As for the issue of diaspora identity, I reckon it as a different concept from cultural identity in that it no longer believes in cultural myth and given discourses. Thus it can work out a way for diasporic groups to get rid of the repetitive identity performances. Then to gain power from other contexts rather than cultural context is assumed as a more feasible way for them to succeed in their diaspora experiences.

Leslie Marmon Silko's novel *Ceremony* provides us with a positive diaspora experience and is analyzed here to elaborate my argument on the problem of diaspora identity. It gives a successful example of the diasporic subject who gets rid of repetitive identity performances through the decolonization of authoritative discourses and positions himself beyond the cultural context with the Ecological realization of nature.

Conclusively, this study manages to show that a successful diaspora experience is the process of individual deconstruction of enforced discourse and reconstruction of self. In this way, it could be helpful to improve the miserable situation for diasporic groups.

Table of Contents

Ⅰ. **Introduction** ······ 1

Ⅱ. **Diaspora and *Ceremony*** ······ 11

1. The Definition of Diaspora ······ 11
2. *Ceremony* as Diasporic Writing ······ 21

Ⅲ. **Reconsidering Diaspora Identity** ······ 26

1. Diaspora and Cultural Identity ······ 26
2. De-essentialism of Diaspora Identity ······ 42
3. Cultural Articulation in Postcolonial Discourse ······ 51
4. Conclusion ······ 61

Ⅳ. *Ceremony*: Under Identity Performance ········· 66

1. Myth of Cultural Identity ········· 68
2. Self-identification Between Two Cultures ········· 71
3. Conclusion ········· 92

Ⅴ. *Ceremony*: Decolonization of Given Discourses and Ecological Reconstruction ········· 95

1. Decolonization of Colonial Discourses ········· 97
2. Ecological Self-realization ········· 113
3. Conclusion ········· 124

Ⅵ. Conclusion ········· 128

Appendix Ⅰ ········· 135

Appendix Ⅱ ········· 145

Bibliography ········· 156

Acknowledgements ········· 171

Ⅰ. Introduction

I began to find interests in the topic of diaspora when I was studying with my advisor on the curriculum of ethnic American literature. The problem of cultural conflicts and assimilation was frequently mentioned during the discussion. Asian Americans as "model minority," boarding school for Indians, the incomplete multicultural education policy, etc. were talked about as unfair phenomena commonly encountered in the U.S. It appears that American ethnics are discriminated against by the mainstream society or in other words the white who take effort to control and manipulate them through cultural assimilation. However, not all minorities conform to the white culture as they planned, and those who believe in neither homeland culture nor hostland culture are deemed as diasporas. I read several literary works written by American ethnic writers and gradually found that cultural identity is one indispensable and crucial element in studying the issue of diasporas. When I started to write the topic of diaspora, I began with the definition of diaspora and then realized that it is a very vague and hard one to comprehend. I learned from Robin Cohen, Khachig Tölölyan, William Safran and many other scholars of diaspora. But as the research was carried forward, I found that if defined from the geographical aspect alone, it might be a little confusing since there are different types of migration and it does not always result in diaspora[①]. The decisive factor to clarify that a movement belongs to exile, immigration or diaspora lies in the psychological or cultural aspect of a subject. Diasporic groups are those who suffered from cultural default and felt nowhere to position themselves as I defined. Consequently, I moved the emphasis of my research to the issue of cultural identity of diasporas.

When more readings and researches were carried on, the focus gradually evolved to the issue of psychological colonization of colonial discourse. Then to the proper solution

① It may also be exile or immigration, and exile or immigration as well stand a chance to result in diaspora.

for diaspora situation which turned to be decolonization or demystification of given discourse, to not the traditional one of finding and subjected to some pre-existing cultural identities. So I eventually decided to choose Leslie Marmon Silko's novel *Ceremony* to illustrate the topic of diaspora and cultural identity. I considered it to be a positive example of diaspora experience. The author Silko is a Native American who wrote texts based on the background of her own dispersing and rootless experiences.

The description in Silko's novel is to some extent different from the traditional diasporic writing. Usually the diasporic group we commonly referred to are associated with the dispersal across space. According to Cipolla (2017), diasporic communities begin in one place, typically glossed as a "homeland," but end up somewhere completely new. Also the notion that migration or movement across different places is emphasized and featured in a typical definition or experience of diaspora. Native Americans, judging from this criterion, lack the geographical movement or immigration because they are indigenous to America. Their diaspora experience takes place in one land and country. The reason for categorizing them as diasporas lies in the fact that they were expelled to different reservations by the invaders which resulted in the situation of homeless and dispersal. So in the case of Native Americans, the dislocation and displacement from psychological aspect is more significant than that from the common aspect of geographical migration, and this is where my emphasis laid on. To define a diaspora experience, it might be confusing by merely considering the dislocation from a geographical perspective. After all, mental displacement is at some point more important and decisive. Though Native Americans still live in the same country (from their original location to reservations), their identifications with Native Indian culture were broken under the invasion of white culture. As a result, they were deprived of the homeland and original cultural identity. This eventually leads to the situation of cultural default. Mental or psychological displacement as far as I am concerned, contributes to the diasporic condition, and that is why I employ *Ceremony* by Leslie Marmon Silko as a piece of diasporic work here to analyze.

However, the cultural identity for categorizing different groups as diasporas or not gradually fell out of my research emphasis with the progressing of the study since it is a concept of essentialism that will by no means be the proper solution for diaspora situations. According to the idea of Bhabha and Barthes, culture is actually constructed discourse, and there is no authenticity and essence of the concept. The identification with homeland or hostland culture is in a sense illusionary and mystified. Therefore, in the end I turned from Hall's idea of cultural identity to other scholars. Hall (1990) defined the cultural identity of diaspora as a dynamic transforming process with some newness constantly adding in a common background of cultural awareness. Though Hall provided us with the new view of positioning diasporas in a transformative way instead of the traditional fixed identity, the definition is still based on recognizing the essentialism of the concept of culture. Then Butler's theory of Performativity inspired me to a new area of research to deny the essence. The author started to search for new possibilities for the identification of diaspora. This book assumes that identity is also performative as Butler argued for gender. That is to say, there is no pre-existing or pre-given cultural identities, and the commonly approved identity is thus the result of performance that are constructed by authorities as social discourses. It is the repetitive and constant identity performance causes diasporic subjects to naturalize the cultural identity they are subject to as real and essential. As a result, this would fall into an endless cyclic repetition, and diasporic groups as the unprivileged could never make their own utterances. The only way for diasporas to be free from given or enforced discourses is to break the binary oppositions, which coincides with Bhabha's idea.

So far, the research has gone to the key point of decolonization of colonial discourse. In postcolonial discourse, as Bhabha states, culture is constructed discourse manipulated or even manufactured by the social authority to control the unprivileged and consolidate its dominant status. However, it is the subtle status of "ambivalence" between the colonizer and the colonized, and the policy of "mimicry" contradiction that finally leads to the collapse of the system of binary oppositions. This finally made it possible for diasporic groups to get rid of the colonial discourse and negotiate in an interstitial space. But the argument of negotiating in a Third Space, which still takes place in the cultural context, is too vague for us to follow. Let's think back on what we had discussed previously on performativity. Since Bhabha's argument has proved the possibility for diasporas to break from the colonization of cultural discourse, and if diasporic subject does not perform the pre-given or violently enforced identities, then what should he / she perform? Also, where could they gain their power from?

Given the studies made above, this book reckons that the solution for diaspora situation lies in other contexts rather than in culture, for culture in postcolonial discourse is always constructive and illusionary. Naess's idea of Deep Ecology suggests a way of ecological reconstruction of self with intrinsic strength and value. This book thinks this may function in relieving the miserable situation of diasporic groups by gaining power from nature. Especially in the case of *Ceremony*, it proves the realization of self can be fulfilled by ecological holism. Nevertheless, it still needs further research.

In discussing the study on diaspora and diaspora identity, this book intends to include six chapters. The first chapter gives an overview or main points of this research which are how my focus develops and moves in the field of diaspora, the study from Hall's idea, Butler and Bhabha, and an exploration of a theoretical background for the text analysed. It will also mention the idea of Deep Ecology for the proper research in the future on the issue of diaspora.

The second chapter mainly involves two sections. Section one introduces the definition of diaspora from the aspect of cultural identification to make it more precise and specific compared with the traditional definition of diaspora concentrating on geographical movements mainly given by Cohen, Tölölyan and Safran. Section two further discusses the text *Ceremony* and the reason it falls into the category of diasporic writing based on the analysis in section one.

The third chapter is the thorough elaboration on the topic of diaspora and cultural identity through ideas of Stuart Hall, Judith Butler and Homi K. Bhabha to lay a theoretical basis for this study. It concludes that diasporic groups should not position themselves in the fixed or illusionary culture context, subject to some given or enforced identities. The successful diaspora experience could only be achieved on a basis of demystification of discourse, by gaining power from other contexts rather than culture to realize and reconstruct themselves.

In the fourth and fifth chapters, the text analysis is initially carried on with Hall and Butler's idea and then turns to Bhabha's argument on postcolonial culture issue and Arne Naess's idea of Deep Ecology. These two chapters discuss the diaspora experience of the protagonist Tayo in Silko's novel *Ceremony* to prove it as a positive and successful example to provide diasporic groups with possibilities to get rid of psychological colonization and gain power from another context. For further discussion, these two chapters respectively analyze the first half and latter part of this novel since the plot shifts from identity searching and performing to the decolonization of pre-given identity which represents the successful transformation of the protagonist. Chapter Four describes how the protagonist Tayo positions himself from the white culture to the Native American culture to strive his self-identification. Chapter Five examines how Tayo extricates himself from colonial discourses and the given identities to reach the status of self-realization. This happens by gaining power from every nature element to recover and reconstruct himself as diaspora.

The sixth chapter makes a summary of the research above to examine it consecutively to a conclusion of this study and puts forward other possibilities of future research.

Diaspora identity, set beyond the context of culture, is reconstructed on a basis of decolonization of colonial discourses to realize the Ecological-self.

Ⅱ. Diaspora and *Ceremony*

1. The Definition of Diaspora

Diaspora is occasionally an overused word for describing those groups of people who dispersed from their homeland because not all movements should be claimed as diaspora. The movements of people took place due to different reasons, underwent different situations and resulted in different conditions, which definitely bear exclusive features that cannot simply be defined as diasporas. According to Robin Cohen (1992), if we simply theorize diasporas as communities living far from their home countries, then diasporas will be just the outcome of continental and international migration. Or as Butler's stated, "If all movements of people do not result in diasporas, what, then, distinguishes diasporas from other movements of people" (Butler, 2001, p. 189). So, diaspora carries much more connotations than simply the performance of movement or resettlement.

The word diaspora is derived from the ancient Greek word *diaspeirein*, meaning dispersion or scattering, and that from *dia-*, "across" and *speirō*, to sow or scatter. Initially, the word diaspora had a specific usage for describing the dispersion of Jews. As William Safran noted, "the exile of the Jews from their historic homeland and their dispersion throughout many lands, signifying as well the oppression and moral degradation implied by that dispersion" (Safran, 1991, p. 83). Diaspora was at the beginning referring to the sufferings of Jewish dispersion, then later it was gradually applied to intend Greek, and African dispersion. Cohen noted that the origin of diaspora in Bible implies diaspora as "the forcible scattering of the indigenous people, perhaps as a form of punishment by God or fate for abandoning the old ways" (Cohen, 1992, p.159). So diaspora has a history and has gone through ages to refer to those groups of people who scattered from the original homeland where their ancestors lived due to different reasons, such as religious, political, economic, cultural, etc. Ever since the late 20th century, the old term of diaspora referring to Jewish dispersion which had the restrictive usage has been frequently used by different categories of people who carry the features of resettlement and relocation to define themselves.

However, the word diaspora can hardly be defined in a clear and thorough way since it carries very subtle connotations. Walker Connor (1986), gave a simple definition of diaspora as the segment of a people living outside their homeland. According to this definition, it would be easy to get confused since it is very broad and vague. The category of "people living outside the homeland" is a huge one since human beings have gone through perpetual movements through history. However, not all movements will turn out to be diaspora. They might become exile groups, immigrants, overseas communities, ethnic and racial minorities. As Khachig Tölölyan notes, this definition does not make clear what a community is made up of[①] or what the members need to "think, feel, experience, or do in order to be considered

① A community could be made up of refugees, exiles, immigrants or diasporans.

as a segment of the transnational people" (Tölölyan, 1996, p.15). James Clifford refers to Safran's definition of diaspora as follows:

> "expatriate minority communities"(1) that are dispersed from an original "center" to at least two "peripheral" places; (2) that maintain a "memory, vision, or myth about their original homeland"; (3) that "believe they are not — and perhaps cannot be — fully accepted by their host country"; (4) that see the ancestral home as a place of eventual return, when the time is right; (5) that are committed to the maintenance or restoration of this homeland; and (6) of which the group's consciousness and solidarity are "importantly defined" by this continuing relationship with the homeland. (Clifford, 1994, pp.304-305)

Safran's definition of diaspora refers to those "expatriate minority communities" whose members share some of the above characteristics. That is to say one does not necessarily need to conform to all these features to construct a diaspora. Cohen (2008) also approved Safran's view and expressed it as the "common features" to signify a diaspora because they are all the time in a process of transformation. Consequently, diasporas will not completely meet all the features and requirements given previously or to the same degree in all settings. But he also claims that there were some repetitions of Safran's definition[①]. These are just the main features that were listed out to constitute a diaspora. All those discussions, though cannot cover every aspect of diaspora situation, were to help understand the concept of diaspora better.

Meanwhile, Cohen provided us with another method to help to delineate a diaspora which were named the "ideal type[②]." "By using a qualifying adjective — victim, labour, imperial, trade and deterritorialized — I have evolved a simple means of typologizing and classifying various diasporas, not by ignoring what they share in common, but by highlighting their most important characteristics" (Cohen, 2008, p.16). Among the five ideal types, victim diaspora is derived from the traditional diaspora of Jews, Africans and Armenians, which is the most classical and typical one. It can also be used to discuss many other diasporas, for instance, Irish and Palestinians, etc. "Many contemporary refugee groups are incipient victim diasporas

---

① Cohen argues that there need some amendments "concerning the evolution and character of the diasporic groups in their countries of exile" (Cohen, 2008, p.6).

② It is the use of the Weberian "ideal type." Ideal is meant to contrast with "real."

but time has to pass to see whether they return to their homelands, assimilate, and mobilize as a diaspora" (Cohen, 2008, p.18). That is to say, diasporas are mobilized and can change over time. After dispersing from a centered home, the diasporic subject might return to homeland or be assimilated to hostland despite the possibility of becoming a diaspora. This book would reckon those who returned to the homeland as exile groups, those who were assimilated to hostland as immigrants and those who found nowhere to locate as diasporas, which will be explained later. However, among these three results of dispersion, the common ground is that certain geographic locations are involved which are respectively homeland and hostland in the process of dispersing and constructing a diaspora. The divergences are the different attitudes towards these elements or locales in forming a diaspora.

So, the geographic location mentioned here is somewhat a basic and simple characteristic for diaspora. What this book means is that there's still a chance that we might confuse diaspora with other kinds of movements by merely following the characteristics or features of diaspora listed above, and a lot of people claim themselves or are reckoned by others as diasporas even though actually they might not be. As Safran states, diaspora "seems increasingly to be used as metaphoric designations for several categories of people — expatriates, expellees, political refugees, alien residents, immigrants, and ethnic and racial minorities" (Safran, 1991, p.83). To some degree, there is no clear boundary between diaspora and some other overseas ethnic communities①. Like what Tölölyan states about ethnic community and diaspora, "mobility is an internal as well as an external characteristic of the contemporary ethnodiaspora" (Tölölyan, 1996, p.18). They are unstable and change from one to another from time to time. Or as mentioned above like what Cohen considers, even though someone was defined as a diasporic subject at some point, he / she might still be changed or mobilized at another point. Jana Evans Braziel and Anita Mannur referred to diaspora as "displaced communities of people who have been dislocated from their native homeland through the movements of migration, immigration, or exile" (Braziel & Mannur, 2003, p.1), which also suggests that diaspora is

① By saying this, this book means that diaspora and other overseas communities were all geographically similar in that they all move from homeland to hostland.

closely related to the movements of exile and immigration. In other words, exile and immigration might just result in diaspora. Obviously, exile, immigrant and diaspora share a lot of features in common. However, can exile groups or immigrants simply be considered as synonyms of diaspora? James Clifford argued that "such narratives are designed to integrate immigrants, not people in diasporas ... It involves dwelling, maintaining communities, having collective homes away from home (and in this it is different from exile, with its frequently individualistic focus)" (Clifford, 1994, pp. 307-308). That is to say, diasporas can neither be considered as exiles nor immigrants. Before delving into a more detailed study on diaspora, the distinctions among exile, immigration and diaspora are supposed to be elaborated in order to get a full and precise concept and connotation of diaspora. As this book mentioned before, geographic location is so basic a criterion that it cannot accurately characterize the concept of diaspora alone and the current typologies are sometimes so broad or one-sided that similar concepts may easily be confused[①]. As a result, this book would like to abandon those typologies that were used to

① For example, it is claimed that diasporas still retain mythology about their homeland, which this book believes should be the characteristic of exiles.

delineate or check diasporas and contrast the three types of movements from the aspect of cultural recognition or identity.

Exiles refer to the group of people who are away from their homeland as fugitives or refugees. Usually they left their home country reluctantly and wished to go back someday. However, it is almost impossible for them to return since there is no permission for them to go back or they may face the risk of imprisonment and punishment upon returning. Exiles neither enjoy their life nor accept the culture or values in host countries. Instead, they always confirm themselves as part of the native culture. Different from exiles, immigrants refer to the group of people who voluntarily move to the host country where they recognize its culture and take effort to become part of it. They want to get rid of their native culture. Besides these two groups, there still exist some people who accept neither the homeland nor hostland culture and they are termed as diasporas. The reason for them to leave their homeland is similar with exiles or immigrants. What differs from the others is that diasporas do not expect to return to their homeland as exiles, nor do they enjoy the life in host country as immigrants. As a result, diasporas do not define themselves as part of homeland nor hostland, but find nowhere to locate themselves spiritually.

Exile groups, immigrants and diasporas carry some distinct features in that they mentally and psychologically hold different attitudes towards homeland and hostland, which can be concluded as whether or not they recognize cultures of homeland or hostland and confirm themselves to be part of them. And since those distinctions among exile, assimilation and diaspora mainly lie in the psychological aspect, this book is more inclined to define diaspora from a psychological and mental level of displacement and relocation. So diaspora here is not restricted to a mere geographic or locational concept. Moreover, it refers to those who suffer from the mental displacement or a more concrete concept — cultural default[①]. Kenny argued that "ask not what a diaspora 'is' but how the term is used and how it produces meaning ... this approach focuses on how new forms of identity and culture are constituted" (Kenny, 2013, p.12). The psychological attitudes or cultural

① By terming the distinguishing feature of diaspora as cultural default, this book means that diasporan group have no mythologies in neither homeland culture (as exiles do) nor hostland culture (as immigrants do). They build their own culture or in other words, they have their own diaspora identity.

consciousness of diasporic groups towards homeland and hostland is to some extent more important and powerful for defining diaspora especially in literature study.

So this book would claim that culture or cultural identity is the key factor and solution that undergoes constant changes and transformations for diasporic groups who face the cultural dilemma and confusion in the process of defining themselves, and this book tends to define diasporas as people dispersed from their original homeland to hostland suffering from cultural displacement, but not mystified in neither homeland nor hostland culture. They have their own locations of culture which will be discussed in the following chapters.

2. *Ceremony* as Diasporic Writing

Ceremony, published in 1977, is the first novel of Leslie Marmon Silko, which is also one of her many representative works. The writing of *Ceremony* shared the similar background with the living experience of the author herself. Silko was born in Albuquerque in 1948, of mixed ancestry — Laguna Pueblo, Mexican, and white (the protagonist in the novel is a mix-blood of Laguna and the white). She grew up in the Laguna Pueblo Reservation, where she lives with her husband and two children. Silko is one of the most important representatives of Contemporary Native American writers. Besides *Ceremony*, other exceptional novels are *Almanac of the Dead* and *Gardens in the Dunes*. She has also written two works of autobiography, *Sacred Water* and *The Turquoise Ledge*; a collection of essays, *Yellow Woman and a Beauty of the Spirit*; and a book of verse, *Laguna Woman*.

Ceremony tells the story about a young Native American, Tayo, who returns to Laguna Pueblo reservation after surviving the World War II and suffers from what appears to be the PTSD (post-traumatic stress disorder). As one of the ethnic minorities, he is increasingly filled with the feeling of estrangement and alienation because he can find consolation neither in the native culture nor in the white society. Other veterans bury themselves in alcohol and senseless violence, while Tayo searches for another way out.

Tayo, the protagonist in Silko's novel *Ceremony*, is a half-breed and has a special experience. To some extent, the conflicts between ethnic groups and the white society are personified in the self-struggle of Tayo. Compared with the native Indians, Tayo bears a more complicated and subtle identity confusion. On the one hand, he is of Indian American descent and grows up in the Native American reservation, but most Indians reject him because of his white blood. In the novel, Auntie always takes him as a shame of the family and he is psychologically abused by Auntie throughout his early years. As he grows up, there are also some of his friends that treat him unfriendly. Only uncle Josiah is willing to accept him. On the other hand, he carries with him the American white blood, and has no idea of whom his father is. The truth is, he is also discriminated against by the white society because of his Indian origin, and obviously he does not have the opportunity to integrate into the mainstream of the white society as well. He is actually facing the problem of cultural default.

"The usual power imbalance of white / native relations has also been aggravated by the war" (Stein, 2002, p.196), which makes the problem of cultural default and identity loss become even more serious. At the time of conscription, the Army recruiter says that "Anyone can fight for America." Citizens with different colors are assembled because they are patriotic, and they are equal. During the war, Tayo is treated fairly, and his experience during the war provides an opportunity for him to define his American citizenship. But after the war, the Indian soldiers are treated unfairly, and they realize that Americans are just taking advantage of them to fight for the country. They are still being rejected and discriminated against by the mainstream society. Alcohol and senseless violence is the choice the returning soldiers made to escape from the suppression of both shell shock and racial discrimination.

In the face of these difficulties, unlike those veterans, Tayo seeks for other solutions to console his feelings of estrangement and alienation. That is the ceremony, through which he eventually gets rid of the identity crisis and renegotiates the relationships with traditional Indian culture and the white culture to reach a status of hybridity.

Ceremony is usually discussed concerning the aspects of trauma, ecocriticism and reconstruction of Native American culture and identity. However, here this book tends to employ the novel as a piece of diasporic writing for the following reason. As this book has mentioned previously, besides geographical dislocation, this book considers psychological displacement as an indispensable factor in defining diaspora. As for the protagonist in this novel, Tayo still lives in the same country, and he is an American citizen, which implies no geographical dislocation of people. But as one of the Native Americans, he is the victim of imperialism and has been driven to live in reservation which is not the original place that Native Americans are born and used to live in. Even though the movement is not typical, Tayo suffers from mental displacement. What he faces is similar to other diasporic groups who experience the cultural conflicts caused by traditional native culture and the white culture, and finds nowhere to locate themselves psychologically. Tayo's mix-blood identity locates him neither in the traditional Laguna culture nor in the white culture because Native Americans consider him as a shame and the white society treats him as an inferior and otherness, which eventually leads to the situation of cultural default. He is not the Laguna or the white, that is to say, he cannot identify himself with Laguna culture or the white culture. So, the protagonist Tayo, facing cultural default and identity loss, is actually in accordance with the characteristics of a diasporic subject that this book discussed in section one. As a result, *Ceremony* is analyzed here from the aspect of diaspora.

Ⅲ. Reconsidering Diaspora Identity

1. Diaspora and Cultural Identity

Diasporas defined here refer to those who suffer from mental displacement when different cultures collide with each other. Diasporic groups cannot find their spiritual place in the culture of both homeland and hostland. That is to say, the dislocation or absence of cultural identity leads to the diaspora situation. Cultural identity is a core element in the formation and evolution of diaspora experience, which has undergone different stages of cognition by decades. Paul Ricoeur (1994) provided us with two types of identities. The first one is "personal identity." It bears the connotation of a fixed and constant identity or character which was given in the background of a specific tradition and geographical circumstance. The second type of identity is termed as "narrative identity," which was built through cultural construction and narration. It emphasizes that constitution of the self was developed through a more constructive way. This cognition of cultural identity stays closer to the popular concept and is approved as a positive one by many critics. As a result of the subversive effects of post-structuralism on identity issue, now cultural identity is considered as something socially constructed and changeable. It is built or created by carefully processed histories and politics as needed①. The traditional view that it is some fixed or unchanged ancestry spirit that people with the same origin hold in common has been questioned and criticized.

Basically, cultural identity cannot be discussed separately from each other, and "identity, then, is simultaneously subjective and social, and is constituted in and through culture." Culture and identity are two "inextricably linked" concepts (Brah, 1996, p. 21). Diasporic groups, bearing with them the identity from their original culture, cannot root themselves in hostland. They are likely to be characterized as

① Cultural identity was constructed depending on the social allocation of politics. More than unstable and unnatural fact, it was even manufactured.

"person 'culturally encapsulated' — as if 'culture' was something entirely separated from lived experience" (Brah, 1996, p.24). The culture of mainstream society is not the permitted place for them to identify with and neither are their origins. Then how come an identity not being "constituted in and through culture?" Suffering from the deep suppression of dominant culture of the mainstream society and drastic clashes from different cultures, they desperately need to search for the identity of diasporas. And that's why the related questions of culture and cultural identity have been talked about thoroughly in postcolonial context for diasporas since the cultural situation acquired more complex features.

In postcolonial context, cultural identity issues have become quite complicated and were given different connotations as a result of imperialism. The colliding of cultures could probably lead to the misunderstanding or misreading of different cultures especially the cultures of the colonized. It is natural for the unprivileged to get trapped in the cultural confusion in colonial circumstances since they cannot make their voices heard during the invasion of all aspects. So Fanon et al. (1963) claims that culture should not be defined by race or ethnicity as colonizers advocated, and the European invaders are all the time enforcing and assimilating the colonized who felt culturally lost with the white culture. That is to say, colonialism is not restricted to a mere geographical scale. Moreover, it aims to manipulate the colonized by ideology or specifically speaking, culture. The racialization of culture is to serve the legitimation of invasion or the assimilation of western culture. This is where Fanon's argument lies that cultural identity should not be separated from, but always stay together with national struggle.

> To believe one can create a black culture is to forget oddly enough that [they] are in the process of disappearing ... There will be no such thing as black culture because no politician imagines he has the vocation to create a black republic. The problem is knowing what role these men have in store for their people, the type of social relations they will establish and their idea of the future of humanity. That is what matters. All else is hot air and mystification. (Fanon et al., 1963, p.169)

In other words, black culture will never come into existence unless there is black republics, and culture can only be secured in the independence of nation. Nationalism is the backbone of Fanon's cultural standpoint①. This is why this book would claim that Fanon's view of culture or cultural identity is built within the scope of nation. The only way for the unprivileged to struggle against the control of the dominant is to fight against colonization to achieve their own cultural identity, or this book would say, their national identity. So, the cultural identity we discussed here is built within the boundaries of nation and upon the people with the same origin, which seems to carry features of stable, fixed and unchangeable. It was given and considered as an identity built within some certain traditions or circumstances.

However, does this kind of cultural identity truly exist? In postcolonial condition, this kind of identity could not survive and was always deemed as a negative one by critics②. Gillian Rose wrote in her essay by concluding Bhabha's idea:

> He introduces his essays by rehearsing the familiar point that now, at the end of the 20th century, many of the interpretive certainties once thought so reliable can no longer be depended upon. The ground has shifted and continues to shift.

---

① Fanon's view on culture served for his nation struggle. It is required for the certain purpose of violent revolution against colonization.

② Because postcolonial situation brings cultural difference and political uncertainties on moments of articulation that fixed identity can no longer depend on.

> Narratives of origin, journey, and destination can no longer be heroic myths of conquest; traditions can no longer be understood as articulating the essence of pure identity; cultural difference can no longer be seen as a panorama of multicultural diversity; class and gender can no longer be used as singular categories. Origin, authenticity, and essence are for Bhabha all dead tropes. (Rose, 1995, p.366)

So, cultural identity no longer bears the connotation of some given and stable traditional authenticity that a group of people share in common and claim themselves to belong to. In postcolonial condition, one would start to realize that the idea of pure culture or identity is on shaky ground and there is no such thing as essential or inherent. When different cultures encounter, different meanings are produced and interpreted. One can no longer count on the consistency of some group or fixed cultural identities. They exist as some regulated or fixed stereotypes which are in line with tradition or custom. Homeland or hostland cultural identity is in this sense fixed, pre-existing and colonized, which is myth actually.

According to ideas of myth①, everything is not real but symbolic since "myth is a type of speech, everything can be a myth provided it is conveyed by a discourse" (Barthes, 2009, p. 131). The so-called cultural identity then is not real, but ideal, symbolic and abstract. And the essence or authenticity of it turns out to be myth or illusion actually②. The desire for homeland or hostland culture of exile and assimilation subjects is an ideal that is contradicted by certain realities that they are the unprivileged group and have been taken advantage of in the system. That is to say, they are colonized by the illusion of certain cultures where myth created by the privileged group stand behind. What this book intends here is that those who confirm themselves as part of one fixed culture identity are actually under the psychological or mental colonization of a certain social discourse. As this book has discussed before, diasporas are different from exile and assimilation groups by definition. Diaspora subjects do not

① According to Roland Barthes, the main purpose of myth is to hide itself to let people unable to notice the existence of it and take everything happening around them for granted. We will discuss the idea of myth in the following chapter.

② Take the wine in Barthes's *Mythologies* as an example. The wine in French society is portrayed or mystified by the bourgeoisie as the symbol of robust, healthy and relaxing despite the fact that it may be to some extent harmful to human body. Cultural identity is the same case.

believe in illusion or myth of both homeland and hostland. They are demystified or decolonized groups of people who stay closer to the truth. That is where the argument lies in. Diasporic groups accept neither homeland nor hostland culture and take effort to create something new which is virtually the decolonization of myth or illusion. In order to get a clear view of diaspora identity, let's start from delving into a more detailed understanding of the concept of identity.

Identity is similar to culture in the sense that, though we talk about it occasionally, we seldom stop to ask what it is. We usually term it as "this identity" or "that identity" and take it for granted that identities are something concrete and real. The truth is, identities are just changing illusions. Avatar Brah (1996) concluded Erikson's idea and claimed that identity is never of anything static and unchangeable.

To provide cultural identity with another vision, Hall (1990) noted that "instead of thinking of identity as an already accomplished fact, which the new cultural practices then represent, we should think, instead, of identity as a 'production' which is never complete, always in process, and always constituted within, not outside, representation[①]" (p.222). That is to say, cultural identity is always in a process of forming and constructing, not under a status of finished or completed. We can never consider it as some completed fact. From the above analysis, we can conclude that cultural identity is not only constructed, but always in a process of constructing.

To get a full view, let's turn to Hall's two positionings of cultural identity. The first positioning emphasizes some common spiritual essence and defines cultural identity "in terms of one, shared culture, a sort of collective 'one true self' hiding inside the many other, more superficial or artificially imposed 'selves', which people with a shared history and ancestry hold in common" (Hall, 1990, p.223). So, by this kind of definition, cultural identity indicates certain groups as stable and fixed people who are not affected by the vicissitudes of history and still believe in some cultural essentialism or continuous ancestry spirit. This kind of cultural identity, in Hall's view, should not be underestimated

① Meanings are conveyed through the representational system of concepts, signs, or images by language. Then identity produced in representation is in fact discourses or concepts which are constructed by social actors.

because it always makes a difference in social movements[①]. What is important is that "not the rediscovery but the production of identity" matters. It is "not an identity grounded in the archaeology, but in the re-telling of the past" (Hall, 1990, p.224). Under this definition, cultural identity signifies an imaginary coherence with the past through representation. It might be separated for some time in history, but once the connections were set in place, the "loss of identity" would begin to heal. We could not say whether this conception of cultural identity is proper; the only thing for sure is that it plays a crucial role in historical experiences and will be possible to function in some future moments of certain position.

The second different positioning of cultural identity is "a matter of 'becoming' as well as of 'being,' not an essence but a positioning," which is a dynamic transforming process with different culture and history constantly intervening for identifying oneself.

Cultural identity, in this second sense, is a matter of

① The social movements refer to feminist, anti-colonial and anti-racist movements. Here this positioning of cultural identity also functions as an important element in Fanon's argument on anti-colonial struggle.

> "becoming" as well as of "being." It belongs to the future as much as to the past. It is not something which already exist, transcending place, time, history, and culture. Cultural identities come from somewhere, have histories. But, like everything which is historical, they undergo constant transformation. Far from being eternally fixed in some essentialized past, they are subject to the continuous "play" of history, culture, and power. Far from being grounded in mere "recovery" of the past, which is waiting to be found, and which when found, will secure our sense of ourselves into eternity, identities are the names we give to the different ways we are positioned by, and position ourselves within, the narratives of the past. (Hall, 1990, p.225)

Through this version of definition, one can better understand the colonial experience. This second positioning argues that cultural identity is constructed not only through "similarity," but some points of "*difference*" as well. One cannot always stand in one fixed position that is already existing in somewhere, instead, with the intervening of history and culture, there are different positions of cultural experiences. Let's discuss it under the postcolonial experience. People start noticing that at the same time there exist some common historical ground and cultural difference when they encounter others of different nation or ethnicity[①]. Cultural identity is not simply some "universal transcendental spirit" inside which history has no profound influences. "It is not once-and-for-all. It is not a fixed origin to which we can make some final and absolute return" (Hall, 1990, p.226). In other words, we might secure our cultural identity once at a certain position in history, but with difference breaking in, one cannot count on the ancestry spirit forever since history is in a continuous way of development that would never end or fix in one position. Cultural identity in this way also signifies other different positions that interrupt the continuity of similarity. It is this rupture or discontinuity that matters in the second positioning of cultural identity.

Bhabha also discussed the problem of cultural identity and he as well considered that the realization of cultural identity is through a series action of construction, not just fixed in one position with one stable identity. In Hall's statements, "Cultural identities are the points of identification, the unstable points of identification or suture, which are made, within the discourses of history and culture. Not an essence

---

① Someone will start considering who he is when he encounters others, and a community starts to treat itself as one when it encounters other communities.

but a *positioning*" (1990, p.226).

Hall's second view of cultural identity is less familiar and more complicated. In his words, "if identity does not proceed in a straight unbroken line from some fixed origin, how are we to understand its formation?" He explained in the case of black Caribbean:

> We might think of black Caribbean identities as 'framed' by two axes or vectors, simultaneously operative: the vector of similarity and continuity; and the vector of difference and rupture ... The one gives us some grounding in, some continuity with, the past. The second reminds us that what we share is precisely the experience of a profound discontinuity. (1990, pp.226-227)

In other words, cultural identity is constructed under the simultaneous interaction of similarity and difference. Similarity is the common cultural experience or some fixed essential spirit from history. Difference is something new and peculiar that breaks in due to some separations. Similarity signifies continuity with the past and difference signifies discontinuity. Difference does not exist separately from similarity and similarity cannot live independently. "Difference, therefore, persists — in and alongside continuity"

(Hall, 1990, p.227). That is how cultural identity formed, through admitting and accepting the discontinuity on the basis of a common ground[①] in history. Hall positioned the cultural identity of Caribbean through the relation of three "presences[②]" based on the concept of difference.

If we put this positioning of cultural identity in some common postcolonial discourse, not just Caribbean, we can explain it in this way. The colonial experience requires the presence of a different culture, together with some original or ancestry cultural spirit. When difference breaks in, different positions of cultural identity appear. However, the positioning is not fixed in one place and last forever. It slides from one position to another and changes with history. What we thought existing in the past and could be secured in the future is no longer the past exactly the same. Cultural identity cannot simply be recovered from the past, instead, it is reconstructed from different positions. We have

---

① Here by saying common ground, Hall refers to the shared history or experience of the group of people who suffered from slavery, exile, colonization and immigration.

② The three "presences" in Hall's statements are, "to borrow Aimee Cesaire's and Leopold Senghor's metaphor: Presence Africaine, Presence Europeenne, and the third, most ambiguous, presence of all — the sliding term, Presence Americaine" (Hall, 1990, p.230).

"become" who we are, not "being" who we are.

The cultural identity Hall intended here is different from the traditional version of cultural identity and bears some connotation of difference and transformation from a certain position. Through this positioning of cultural identity, we could think of the diaspora experience once again. Hall noted:

> The diaspora experience as I intend it here is defined, not by essence or purity, but by the recognition of a necessary heterogeneity and diversity; by a conception of 'identity' which lives with and through, not despite, difference; by *hybridity*. Diaspora identities are those which are constantly producing and reproducing themselves anew, through transformation and difference. (1990, p.235)

That is to say, diasporic groups are not those who claim themselves to belong to some fixed, pure and ancestry spirit. On the contrary, they belong to the group of people who can see through cultural politics in colonial situation and always have a clear insight on the constructed discourses. As this book has mentioned before, diasporas are different groups of people from exile and assimilation. Diasporic groups will not be sophisticated with essentialism of fixed identity that was located or positioned in one place. They know where they came from and have a definite positioning of themselves. They understand that their diaspora experiences were constructed through the hybridity of difference and underwent constant transformations. Thus diaspora identity is not the group identity but a kind of individual identity for the recognition of heterogeneity[①] (Lowe, 1991). Every diasporic individual has different historical experiences and he or she should not be classified into some certain categories. That is why we say diasporic groups are not subject to the absolute identification of homeland or hostland culture. They construct and reproduce their own cultural identity through difference and hybridity.

So, Hall's idea provides us with some possibilities to understand and clarify the concept of diaspora and diaspora identity from other terms whose groups share some similar experiences and characteristics. It claims that cultural identity is a dynamic transforming process and formed through similarity and difference, which acknowledges the existing

① Lisa Lowe argued the importance of heterogeneity by saying that Asian Americans should not be simply classified as one category since they all carried with them distinct characteristics politically, socially, economically and culturally.

and authenticity of cultural identity. For Hall, even though diasporas will not be trapped in some fixed identity, they still believe in the essentialism of identity. That is to say, cultural identity is constructed somewhere already existing for people to choose and claim themselves to belong to. However, will this formation and authenticity of identity function successfully in the diaspora experience? If we reconsider it under Butler's theory of Performativity, we might find that answers are different.

2. De-essentialism of Diaspora Identity

We have discussed that diaspora identity is different from those fixed positioning of inherent ancestry spirit, which suggests that there exist some pure and group culture diasporas belong to. Diaspora identity is constructed through a dynamic transforming process, that never fixed in one position, but formed under the simultaneous functions of similarity and difference. It was naturally deemed as real and pre-existing. However, by conforming to some certain identities, diasporas may easily get trapped in the mist of essentialism, since the concept of identity was given and enforced by authoritative discourses. Thus this book believes

Butler's theory of Performativity may bring new thoughts and ideas on the issue of diaspora. She also notes that a few scholars have extended Performativity theory to the study of racial problems①. So this section would try to discuss it with diaspora identity here.

Judith Butler was influenced by Austin② in the proposition of her idea of gender performativity. Austin believes that there is no authentic gender or ontology, and it is the result of performance. Butler noted that:

> Such acts, gestures, enactments, generally construed, are *performative* in the sense that the essence or identity that they otherwise purport to express are *fabrications* manufactured and sustained through corporeal signs and other discursive means. That the gendered body is performative suggests that it has no ontological status apart from the various acts which constitute its reality. (2006, p.185)

In other words, there is no pre-existing gender, and we

---

① Scholars such as Saidiya Hartman, Lisa Lowe and Dorinne Kondo have made such researches. If Butler's idea of gender performativity can explain other relative problems, it is likely to function under multiple related backgrounds.

② J. L. Austin, in *How to Do Things with Words*, made two categories of utterances — constative utterance and performative utterance. He defined performative utterance not only as "saying" something, but as "doing" something, and it leads to an action with words.

believe in some kind of "essential" gender trait, which is actually the result of social norms constantly acting on our bodies. We are just performing the pre-given gender as naturally inherent. Butler also noted:

> I wondered whether we do not labor under a similar expectation concerning gender, that it operates as an interior essence that might be disclosed, an expectation that ends up producing the very phenomenon that it anticipates. In the first instance, then, the performativity of gender revolves around this metalepsis, the way in which the anticipation of a gendered essence produces that which it posits as outside itself. Secondly, performativity is not a singular act, but a repetition and a ritual, which achieves its effects through its naturalization in the context of a body, understood, in part, as a culturally sustained temporal duration. (2006, xv)

Therefore, gender does not exist prior to social discourse. In fact, it is the result of discourse construction. Gender is formed in some continuous behavioral production, which is constrained by discourse rules and practices. The "inherent essence" of gender is actually the repetition of a series of acts subordinate to gender norms. What we deemed to be real and authentic is merely the naturalization of the certain context and "the naturalized knowledge of gender operate[ing] as a preemptive and violent circumscription of reality." It is the anticipation of essence that in turn produces what we regard as "real." The "real" us are in fact not real but the hallucination of the realization of our anticipations. So, behind the expression of gender, there is no gender ontology. Gender is formed in the continuous and repetitive performances. There is first performance, then gender identity①.

To make it clearer, we can find that Butler once noted that ever since 16, **being** a lesbian is what she has been. To be someone is not to be **being** someone. To be someone admits ontology. Being someone is like taking up a role. That is her defense, and she assumes there's no ontology or authentic self. She doubts that women exist as a stable category, instead it is a process of being a woman. She stated that:

> When such categories come into question, the reality of gender is also put into crisis: it becomes unclear how to distinguish the real from the unreal. And this is the occasion in

① That is what performativity argues; it assumes that performance precedes the subject, and the subject gets its meaning in the process of performance. But performance actually presupposes that there is someone (a subject) who is performing his or her gender. So for performance, there is pre-existing subject and it is authentic and real.

> which we come to understand that what we take to be "real," what we invoke as the naturalized knowledge of gender is, in fact, a changeable and revisable reality. (2006, xxiv)

Physiological gender is not a "body state in the conscious construction of social gender, but a cultural form that controls the authentic body." Gender is never real, it is the naturalization of certain knowledge that makes us take it as real. For Butler, gender is a constructive idea that is repeated over time. It is not a simple fact or a static state of the body, but a process.

Butler also criticized and denied the authenticity or originality of privileged gender roles by using Derrida's idea of *Differance*[①]. In Butler's case, she argues that it is not necessary that heterosexual precedes homosexual, and there is no reason that heterosexual is original. You cannot have the concept of heterosexual without the concept of homosexual. They are mutually dependent on each other, and there should be no questions of who came first, and they are always already

---

① See http://openmedia. yale. edu/projects/courses/spring09/engl300/mp3/engl300_23_041409.mp3, the example of "the raw," "the cooked," Queer theory and gender performativity. By saying that there is a raw carrot, it implies that there also exist cooked carrots. The only way you know the carrot is raw is because it can be or had not been cooked.

there together. It is the same case with gender and drag[①]. Drag comes along and parodies, mimics, and imitates gender, but what it points out is that gender is always in and of itself precisely performance.

What we discussed above about the performative attribute of gender "shows that what we take to be an internal essence of gender is manufactured through a sustained set of acts, posited through the gendered stylization of the body" (Butler, 2006, xv). That is the negation of the "internal essence of gender." Besides this, Butler also made some other arguments outside the scope of gender, that "what we take to be an 'internal' feature of ourselves is one that we anticipate and produce through certain bodily acts, at an extreme, an hallucinatory effect of naturalized gestures" (2006, xv-xvi). In other words, the naturalization of certain norms and discourses into the internal essence is not merely restricted in gender performativity. Butler also extended her idea of performativity by using Althusser's *Interpellation* to argue that subject does not exist prior to

① Here drag is an example to prove that "reality" is not as invariable and fixed as we generally considered it to be. Instead, it is variable and fragile. It aims to break the gender norms imposed and enforced compulsorily and violently on us.

discourse, but subject to the performativity of discourse, through *interpellating*.

> Thus this is no 'I' who stands behind discourse and executes its volition or will through discourse. On the contrary, the 'I' only comes into being through being called, named, interpellated, to use the Althusserian term, and this discursive constitution takes place prior to the 'I'; it is the transitive invocation of the "I". (Butler, 2011, p.171)

The view that there exists something internal and authentic can no longer be counted on. This provided possibilities for us to question the authenticity of diaspora identity and the internal or inherent characteristics and essentialisms of a subject. You thought "you" bear exclusive feature or internal spirit that can differentiate yourself from somebody else. But this is not the feature or spirit that makes "you". You are only performing and naturalizing the feature or spirit to become "you".

From the above analysis, can we presume that performance produces identity① or diaspora? You can perform an identity

① It is similar to Foucault's idea. Foucault argues that discourse creates power-knowledge, power-knowledge creates identity, and knowledge circulated and imposes its effect on us or our behavior we perform.

by repeating, imitating and parodying in drag. An identity is just one's construct towards being a self, which is naturalized through repetitive performances. Here is the way it works: I am insecure of all the things because I keep performing, and I keep repeating what I suppose myself to be, a perpetual self-construction which does two things at once. It stabilizes my identity which is its intention. But at the same time, it betrays my anxiety about my identity in that I must perpetually repeat it to keep it going[①]. It is the repetitive and continuous performance makes you to fulfill the identification of "you" as a subject in process.

Here I would like to lend two main points from Butler's theory of Performativity. Firstly her theory on gender. She argues that there's no internal or authentic pre-existing gender or ontology. The reality of gender is the result of repetitive naturalization of performances. Secondly, she tries to break the binary oppositions with Derrida's *Différance* of women / inferior and men / superior, which shares some similarities with Bhabha's idea on culture. If we consider diaspora issue under the mechanism of the two points, we

---

① Also see http://openmedia.yale.edu/projects/courses/spring09/engl300/mp3/engl300_23_041409.mp3.

may find something interesting. Generally speaking, we tend to treat people as a certain category because they bear certain identity. The identities they carry determine who they are. So diasporas are diaspora because their identities claim them to be diaspora. However, in Butler's case, there should be no pre-existing identity which is internal and essential. The so-called "real" identity is the naturalization of repetitive performances of social discourses and norms. For diaspora, diaspora identity is performative and should not exist prior to diasporic subjects. Thus diasporas are diaspora in that they were compulsory and violently enforced by cultural authority and social discourse as diaspora. When unfettered by the bound of discourses, they can build the demystified selves of diasporas, not the socially enforced "diasporas." That is to say, diasporic groups will not be trapped by some constructed discourses given by the authority as cultural politics, which were acted on again and again to let them believe they are real, authentic and pre-existing. So diasporic subjects should find their way through breaking the authoritative cultural discourses, not by being subjected to some identities.

3. Cultural Articulation in Postcolonial Discourse

Culture, as Avtar Brah termed, "may be viewed as the symbolic construction of the vast array of a social group's life experiences"(1996, p.18). It carries with it the images of values, customs, traditions that were marked by histories in different stages. So, "cultures are never static: they evolve through history. That is why the process of cultural reproduction is, in part, a process of cultural transformation" (Brah, 1996, p.18). With history constantly intervening, culture receives the new meanings at certain positions and transforms from time to time. That's why we say culture will never be static since history and human continue.

Bhabha also denied the kind of ancestral and originated stable culture. Instead, he chose to believe in a contradicted and ambivalent cultural status. He set this in the background of the minority group who were ignored or taken advantage of by others[①]. What they face was, in postcolonial condition, the dominated and hegemonic class who took

① Here Bhabha illustrated this problem on the basis of his own experience of a minority when living in a society that were ignored or forgotten by the mainstream. And that's where he goes beyond the binary oppositions and sees through the discourses.

control of the social discourse aimed to colonize them on cultural aspect. As the unprivileged group in society, they have little choice of constructing their cultural identity. According to Bhabha, it was precisely locating in this cultural dilemma and suffering from the cultural ambivalence that led them to locate in the culture of the liminal space which grows beyond the boundaries of dualistic oppositions of Self and Other.

> It is in the emergence of the interstices — the overlap and displacement of domains of difference — that the intersubjective and collective experiences of *nationness*, community interest, or cultural value are negotiated. (Bhabha, 1994, p.2)

The cultural meanings and differences are negotiated in-between, and the negotiation can only be carried on in an interstitial space. Bhabha argues that there is no such culture that was produced as traditional or pure in postcolonial discourse. When different cultures encounter, the interrelation of the dominant and others is not simply agonistic. They bleed into each other and make articulations of something new[1].

In order to get a better understanding of the interactions of different cultures, let's take a look at Bhabha's idea on

---

[1] This "bleed-into each other" is not the simple combination of different cultures, but the negotiation and articulation of difference.

culture:

> What is theoretically innovative, and politically crucial, is the need to think beyond narratives of originary and initial subjectivities and to focus on those moments or processes that are produced in the articulation of cultural difference. (Bhabha, 1994, p.1)

Obviously, Bhabha's argument was based on the concept of cultural difference. Here the term cultural difference signifies some underlying implications other than simply different cultures. So Bhabha made a distinction between terms of cultural difference and cultural diversity. Usually, we found little distinctions between these two terms. But in this case by emphasizing the unique value of cultural difference, Bhabha laid the basis for his theory:

> This revision of the history of critical theory rests, I have said, on the notion of cultural difference, not cultural diversity. Cultural diversity is an epistemological object — culture as an object of empirical knowledge — whereas cultural difference is the process of the *enunciation* of culture as 'knowledgeable', authoritative, adequate to the construction of systems of cultural identification. (1994, pp.49-50)

In Bhabha's view, cultural diversity and cultural difference are two ways to describe culture in postcolonial discourse, which are to some extent opposed to each other by implication and value.

Cultural diversity is the "recognition of pre-given cultural contents and customs." It is likely to lead to the consolidation of different cultures and admit the essentialism of culture. To embrace multiculturalism is to comfort oneself safely in "the Utopianism of a mythic memory of a unique collective identity." So, cultural diversity suggested that cultures lived unaffectedly and "unsullied by the intertextuality of their historical locations" (Bhabha, 1994, p.50). What Bhabha emphasized is that the interrelationship between colonial discourse and mainstream culture is not merely antagonistic. The statement of cultural diversity just makes it excessively stabilized and essential.

On the contrary, the statement of cultural difference implies a more fluid and flexible interrelationship among cultures or discourses. And it was described as resisting the colonial cultural authority. Meanwhile the language of the master becomes hybrid in the practice of domination. In postcolonial discourse, cultural difference claims a kind of misreading or misappropriated using of signs. This would produce the ambivalence and instability of discourse when the cultural disturbances of the colonized break in on the level of enunciation, and the ambivalence here successfully deconstructed the dualistic antagonism between the colonizer and the colonized. In other words,

> The concept of cultural difference focuses on the problem of the ambivalence of cultural authority: the attempt to dominate in the name of a cultural supremacy which is itself produced only in the moment of differentiation. And it is the very authority of culture as a knowledge of referential truth which is at issue in the concept and moment of *enunciation*. (Bhabha, 1994, pp.50-51)

To make it simple, the dominant status of the colonizer is no longer stable in front of the disturbance and narration of the colonized since they produce "an unresolvable problem of cultural difference for the very address of colonial cultural authority." So let's turn to the "problem of the ambivalence of cultural authority" and the influence it has on the binary opposition system in postcolonial discourse.

In the background of Bhabha's postcolonial theory, the word "ambivalence" was used to describe the complicated relations and status between the colonizer and the colonized. The colonizer always thought their culture as refined, advanced and superior, while the culture of the colonized as barbaric, underdeveloped and backward. And they felt a great sense of mission to educate and civilize the colonized as they wished. So they carried out the strategy of "mimicry", which was a control form for the colonizer to control the colonized not only by mimicking their extrinsic appearance, action or behavior, but also the inherent culture or values. However, it did not progress as they expected. Taking the colonized India as an example, what does the mimicry strategy aims to construct, the true Englishman or just English mimics? If it were the true Englishman, then the colonizer would lost their superior position compared with the inferior colonized since they were identical both extrinsically and intrinsically. If it were the English mimics, then it would be a failure of the educating and civilizing mission since the culture status of the colonized were still underdeveloped and far from being refined or advanced. Obviously as long as the colonizer insists that there must be differences existing between the colonizer and the colonized, the strategy of mimicry would never work out. Then it would fall into the ambivalent status, which also broke the authority of the colonial discourse because of the enunciation and disturbances of differences made by the colonized. Thus the binary divisions of superior and inferior, center and edge, East and West were at the same time surpassed.

This significant status of ambivalence between colonial subjects in Bhabha's consideration will eventually lead to the collapse of the colonial cultural authority. And it implies that the binary division between the colonizer and colonized will sooner or later be interrupted and broken regardless of whether the attitude is acquiescent or oppositional of the colonized subject. Moreover, Bhabha believes that the incomplete mimicry policy also reveals the internal conflict of the colonial authority, which then contributes to the collapse of its authoritative status. Unsurprisingly, ambivalence results in the non-centralization of the colonial cultural authority and subversion of the dualistic oppositions of the colonizer and colonized. And the interrelations between colonial subjects that went beyond the dualistic oppositions opened up new cultural spaces for them to negotiate in. These are places where difference flow into each other and something new that Bhabha terms as hybrid is articulated:

> The process of cultural hybridity gives rise to something different, something new and unrecognizable, a new area of negotiation of meaning and representation. (Bhabha, 1990, p.211)

That is to say, hybridity predicates a status of colliding and communicating between different cultures instead of independent agon①. And it also bears the intention of resistance to the subversive postcolonial discourse. G. Rose wrote in her essay:

> This hybrid newness is for Bhabha the subversive postcolonial. The hybrid is not conceptualized as a third term which can synthesize the dualism of same and other, though; rather, it is a term which radically disrupts that dualism by articulating its contradictions, thus estranging the dominant culture's rules of recognition. (1995, p.367)

Hybridity, then, provides a way to dispel the dualistic oppositions of culture, where the colonizer disparages the colonized as fetishism. To make it clearer, the colonizer asserts the inferiority in aspects of ethic, civilization and religion of the colonized, and the invasion and colonization is

① Bhabha extended the use of hybridity to the group of diaspora and immigrant to refer to a kind of contamination of the purity.

for the purpose of normalizing and civilizing of them. Nevertheless, if the colonized were able to be normalized or civilized, and became what the colonizer considered as superior, then the inferiority would not be a kind of inherent or essential property. Thus it turned out to be some acquired social discourses. So, problems such as misunderstanding or discomforting would occur at the moment when different cultures collide with each other. However, culture by essence does not exist, and the presence of culture is a kind of discourse which is created and told by the dominant again and again as politics. Hybridity then provided an in-between space for different cultures to enunciate and negotiate. Bhabha notes:

> Hybridity to me is the 'third space' which enables other positions to emerge. This third space displaces the histories that constitute it, and set up new structures of authority, new political initiatives. (1990, p.211)

The negotiating is carried out in a way that "disrupts that dualism by articulating its contradictions," not "synthesises," narrates something new, not dualistic opposition, and deconstructs the discourse, not naturalizes.

Culture or cultural identity is also reconstructed through

hybridity and the relation is renegotiated consequently. And that happens in certain "contact zones." As G. Rose wrote in her essay:

> Bhabha's demand for cultural difference demands a different spatiality: not a hybridity between same and other. This would be a space of tension, neither one nor the other, an interstitial space of discontinuity and disjuncture through which the newness of hybrid identities could be articulated. A space which, in the eyes of dominant contemporary theorizing, must seem obscure indeed. (1995, p.369)

The place of utterance in Bhabha's view that carries the feature of hybrid and ambivalence is interstitial or in-between. It is termed as the Third Space. In Third Space, new meanings and discourses were produced by cultural translation. Cultures were no longer considered as pre-given and stabilized essentialism because "cultures are never unitary in themselves, nor simply dualistic in the relation of Self and Other." Bhabha also claims:

> It is only when we understand that all cultural statements and systems are constructed in this contradictory and ambivalent space of enunciation, that we begin to understand why hierarchical claims to the inherent originality or 'purity' of cultures are

> untenable, even before we resort to empirical historical instances that demonstrate their hybridity. (1994, pp.54-55)

That is to say, the interrelations between different cultures are not always restricted in a dualistic opposition, and cultures should not be claimed as some pre-given, original and pure essentialism. In fact, when different cultures encounter, it becomes ambivalent and hybrid. The cultures can no longer keep independently separated. On the contrary, they start to cross over the boundaries of solidity and flow in the "contact zone." The difference between different cultures will lead to the ambivalences at the edge of communicating and eventually the subversion of postcolonial discourses. Thus with the non-centralization of the colonial cultural authority, cultures were no longer considered as inherent but constructed for the colonial authority to maintain the hierarchical order as politics. Those who noticed the mechanism then could negotiate in the interstitial space, and see through the cultural mist of colonialism to build the self.

4. Conclusion

In conclusion, this chapter would like to try to discuss issues of diaspora and diaspora identity in the following aspects.

Diaspora, in the first place, should be defined not merely on a geographical level, but from the mental and psychological aspect, in terms of culture. Previously this book has defined diaspora as people living outside their homeland, mentally displaced or dislocated, meanwhile suffering from cultural confusion or identity default. So cultural identity becomes a crucial element in diaspora experiences.

In Hall's idea, diaspora experience is not defined by essence or purity, but by "the recognition of a necessary heterogeneity and diversity," through difference and hybridity. And identity is built with two axes and vectors of continuity and difference. It is a dynamic transforming process instead of some fixed ancestry spirit. So can we assume this as the diaspora identity? It seems that the identity constructed here is likely to be considered as diaspora identity. However, even though Hall denied the fixed or group identity, he still believed in the concept of identity which is real and pre-existing for diasporas to conform to and locate themselves in. This is the limitation of Hall's idea on identity. Claiming the authenticity of identity may easily lead to the failure of diaspora experience. So when we take Butler's theory of Performativity into consideration, it will provide us with possibilities of a more in-depth thinking on the issue of diaspora and diaspora identity.

Performativity has provided us with a different view to reconsider the problem of diaspora — there is no essentialism or ontology of diaspora identity. Identity is not pre-existing for you to perform, instead what you performed were naturalized social discourses enforced by authority as identities to let you believe they are real and authentic. This book reckons "diaspora identity[①]" as a process of individual deconstruction of social discourse and reconstruction of self. For diasporas, it is the performances made them diasporas, not the violently enforced diaspora identity carried out by social authority. To get rid of the enforced identity, they need to figure out the way to break or collapse the authoritative culture of colonial discourse since identity was built through culture.

In postcolonial discourse, Bhabha argues that culture

① Here the "identity" is not the identity that was constructed through authoritative discourses to enforce on diasporas, but an identity secured by diaspora discourse and getting its power through something else. It is not pre-existing, but come naturally as a result.

should no longer be deemed as something pure, essential or inherent. Culture in postcolonial discourse is constructed through difference. The ambivalence of cultural difference breaks the binary opposition of the colonizer and the colonized and opens up a Third space for them to negotiate. New meanings and discourses are produced and enunciated through cultural hybridity. Thus there's a chance for the minority or unprivileged not to be manipulated by the authoritative discourses that are usually enforced on them. In the case of diasporas, uncontrolled by the authoritative discourse, they no longer need to perform their enforced identity, then what should they perform?

The author will briefly introduce this book's assumption here and explain detailedly when analyzing it with the text of *Ceremony*. Since cultural discourse is deemed as constructed and illusionary, it can no longer provide diasporas with possibilities to get rid of colonial discourses. Cultural context will consequently lead diasporic groups to a repetitive performances of pre-given identities. To get rid of enforced identity, diasporas need not only to break the psychological colonization of authoritative discourses but to gain power from other context rather than culture. According to Naess

(1995), Self can be realized through the interrelationship of every natural element. Diasporas will find themselves in the wholeness of ecological system. That is to say, nature, instead of culture, is likely to provide diasporic groups with another context to build and reconstruct themselves unfettered by colonial discourses.

Ⅳ. *Ceremony*: Under Identity Performance

In this chapter, the emphasis goes to the analysis of Leslie Marmon Silko's novel *Ceremony*. As the plot of this novel shifts from identity searching and performing to the decolonization of given identities of the protagonist, this chapter will focus on the first half of this novel and mainly analyzes the process of identity searching and performing of the protagonist Tayo. Section one gives a brief explanation of the myth of cultural identity. If culture is constructed through discourses, then why would people constantly and repetitively perform it naturally without noticing its illusionism? That's because myth stands behind those discourses. Section two describes Tayo's identity performance of the two positionings of culture. It starts from Tayo and those veterans who survive the warfare and come back to Laguna, then mainly deals with the protagonist's searching and conforming to certain identities. Both Tayo and the veterans are suffering from cultural default and identity loss, so they are anxious to set themselves in some certain cultural context and conform to the given identities. At the beginning, Tayo wants to identify himself with the white culture as other veterans do, but eventually failed. Then, Tayo turns to the Laguna tradition for help. He starts to count on the traditional native culture which coincides with Hall's first positioning of cultural identity, but eventually finds it's not enough to cure his "sickness." The scalp ceremony carried out by the old medicine man Ku'oosh lacks something new for Tayo to get fully recovered. Then he turns to Betonie, who is, similar to Tayo, also a half-breed. He leads Tayo to the ceremony with something new adding in, namely the white culture besides the traditional cure of Native American culture, which coincides with Hall's second positioning of culture identity. This is so far the dynamic transforming process of Tayo's self-identification. However, the ceremony is still not complete. This is the exploration period for Tayo to search for his identity, which turns out to be incomplete and unsuccessful for his repetitive performance of certain identity.

1. Myth of Cultural Identity

We have made some discussions in previous chapter that since the cultural problem in postcolonial period has acquired more complex features, we can no longer count on the traditional standpoint of culture. That is to say, culture is never of anything stable and fixed. It is socially constructed and carefully processed as politics needed. So it changes and sometimes is manufactured according to the prevailing authoritative social discourses. Identity is the same case since it is just "changing illusion."① If cultural identity is just socially constructed discourses, why would people take it as essential and authentic and subject to it as something naturally take place?

This section would reckon that the cultural discourses are myth② since "myth helps to naturalize particular worldviews." And "everything can be a myth provided it is

---

① Avatar Brah (1996) claimed that identity is never of anything static and unchangeable.

② Here "myth" refers to the concept proposed by Roland Barthes. He defined myth as "a type of speech" and "a mode of signification, a form." It is closely related to what Saussure postulated previously under the name of *semiology*.

conveyed by a discourse." The intention of myth is to hide itself and let people take it as natural and for granted. So "myth is experienced as innocent speech: not because its intentions are hidden — if they were hidden, they could not be efficacious — but because they are naturalized" (Barthes, 2009, p.155). Thus the privileged people in society can easily take advantage of myth to make the unprivileged people believe it is natural other than something that is created by those who stand behind to manipulate others. Or we could say this is how cultural discourse is considered as social reality for people to accept and comply with.

Myth is based on the tri-dimensional pattern which are the signifier, the signified and the sign respectively[①]. It is "*a second-order semiological system*" in that "it is constructed from a semiological chain which existed before it" (Barthes, 2009, p. 137). So myth or mythical system is a second language which is built on the linguistic system existing before it. Since the signifier of mythical system bears two

① Also from Saussure's semiological system of language. The signified is the concept; the signifier is the acoustic image; the sign refers to the relation between concept and image.

possibilities which are meaning and form separately[①]. The reading of myth turned out to receive different types. The successful reading of myth requires the "inextricable whole made of meaning and form" to pass from semiology to ideology. Or myth will be destroyed if we read the signifier in a different way, say focus on an empty signifier or a full signifier, which may lead to the result of cynical or demystifying. Then how can myth make its way out of this dilemma?

> The elaboration of a second-order semiological system will enable myth to escape this dilemma: driven to having either to unveil or to liquidate the concept, it will *naturalize* it. (Barthes, 2009, p.154)

So myth is received by transforming history into nature. And the reason why people take it innocently is that they always see myth as "an inductive system" instead of "a semiological system." In other words, myth is read as "a factual system" where people take the signification[②] as facts. And that's why

① Barthes gives two names of the signifier in myth since it can be looked at from two aspects: if we take it as the final term of the linguistic system, we call it *meaning*; if we take it as the first term of mythical system, we call it *form*.

② The third term in mythical system, which is the *sign* in the linguistic system.

certain discourses were considered by people as something authentic and natural. People cannot see through the semiological system inside certain discourse of cultural identity; as a matter of fact, they always take it authentically as historical facts. Thus explained the question why people accept the mythical speech as natural and real without noticing the fact that it is constructed and manufactured. Then let's continue with the analysis of the protagonist's experience in the novel.

2. Self-identification Between Two Cultures

In Silko's novel *Ceremony*, the protagonist, Tayo is a half-breed of Native American and the white. When returning from hospital of wartime as a veteran, he is deeply obsessed with the paralysis of memory, nightmares and fragmentations of reality. Returning to the Laguna Pueblo reservation only intensifies his feeling of estrangement and alienation. He is not accepted by both Native American culture and the white culture. The Native Americans represented by his Auntie take him as a shame because of his absent white father, and the white society also reject him for his Indian blood. As Hall noted that "To return to the

Caribbean after any long absence is to experience the shock of the 'doubleness' of similarity and difference" (1990, p.227), Tayo's return to Laguna causes him to encounter the problem of identity loss of both cultures. As a result, he is eager to locate himself in a certain culture.

This section will start with the exploration of protagonist's attempt to identify himself with the white culture. As one of the Native Americans who suffered from the white assimilation, Tayo was inevitably influenced by the white culture. Especially after being recruited in the army to fight for the U.S., he and many other Indian soldiers were treated equally together with the white. They once got the illusion that they already turned "white" as they thought:

> One time there were these Indians, see. They put on uniforms, but their hair. They went off to a big war. They had a real good time, too. Bars served them booze, old white ladies on the street smiled at them. At Indians, remember that, because that's all they were. Indians ... they had as much as they wanted too. They were MacArthur's boys; white whores took their money as same as anyone. These Indians got treated the same as anyone: Wake Island, Iwo Jima. They got the same medals for bravery, the same flag over the coffin. (Silko,

1986, pp.41-42)

All these signs showed that there was no difference between the Indian soldiers and the white. They could get everything they wanted and received what they deserved with no prejudices from anyone. They sacrificed and fought for this country as part of her. However, until the war ended and they no longer served in the army, they took off the uniforms and found by then that they had been all the time getting their treatment and respect from the uniforms they wore, not them. All those good times they enjoyed were illusionary, the fact was:

> All of a sudden that man at the store waits on you last, makes you wait until all the white people bought what they wanted. And the white lady at the bus depot, she's real careful now not to touch your hand when she counts out your change. You watch it slide across the counter at you, and you know. (Silko, 1986, p.42)

That the war stopped woke these Indians from their illusion of being one of the white society and brought out the fact that they were still discriminated against by the white. They were told by the recruiter before joining the army to show their love for the country, and they could fight for her. But things turn out to be that the white are just taking advantage of them. The even treatment for these Indian soldiers has gone with their uniforms, and they never acquire their identities in the white culture. However, these veterans who find easy refuge in alcohol are reluctant to be excluded by the white society:

> Here they were, trying to bring back that old feeling, that feeling they belonged to America the way they felt during the war. They blamed themselves for losing the new feeling; they never talked about it, but they blamed themselves just like they blamed themselves for losing the land the white people took. They never thought to blame the white people for any of it; they wanted white people for their friends. They never saw that it was the white people who gave them that feeling and it was white people who took it away again when the war was over. (Silko, 1986, p.43)

Not seeing through colonial discourse, they always dream of becoming a member of the white society. The truth is that as colonizers, the white will not accept the colonized Indian as equal subjects without difference. What they seek is the superiority and authority towards the Native American. So wanting "white people for their friend" is just a dream that will never come true. Trapped in the impasse, those veterans could only turn to the alcohol for comfort and to paralyze themselves from the reality of identity loss.

Nevertheless, the protagonist Tayo is not affected by these returning soldiers. He is aware of the fact that as a Native American, it is impossible for him to integrate into the white culture. That his nausea cannot be cured by the white doctor is an expression of his exclusion from the white culture. So he turns to the traditional Laguna culture for help. In the beginning, he is still not accepted when he stays at Auntie's:

> He lay there with the feeling that there was no place left for him; he would find no peace in that house where the silence and the emptiness echoed the loss. (Silko, 1986, p.32)

Auntie is the representative of old Laguna tradition, and her abnegation of Tayo shows the nonacceptance of him by the Native American because of his shamed and disgraceful status of mixed-blood. This is how Auntie has always been treating him. She intentionally makes distinctions between Tayo and her son Rocky to let Tayo notice that he is excluded and aware of the distances between them. So the disconnection of Tayo and the Laguna tradition appeared ever since his childhood. Even when grandma wants to send for a medicine man to help Tayo, Auntie still shows her anger and disagreement.

To reconnect Tayo with the old Laguna tradition, the old medicine man Ku'oosh takes his "Indian medicine" with him to Tayo and starts the healing by talking to him about the old-time stories:

> He spoke softly, using the old dialect full of sentences that were involuted with explanations of their own origins, as if nothing the old man said were his own but all had been said before and he was only there to repeat it. (Silko, 1986, p.34)

What Ku'oosh is trying to do is to connect Tayo with the Native American culture by recalling the old times and memories. The way he talks is like the repeating of history, which gradually recalls Tayo of his childhood in Laguna. The reappearance of history gives Tayo the feeling of belonging to the old Laguna reservation. This section will borrow from Hall's idea of two positionings on the issue of cultural identity to discuss Tayo's ceremony carried out by Ku'oosh.

Hall's first positioning of cultural identity as discussed in the second chapter refers to the fixed and stabilized identity that people with shared history claim to belong to.

Hall has noted that by this definition of cultural identity, "our cultural identities reflect the common historical experiences and shared cultural codes which provide us, as 'one people', with stable, unchanging, and continuous frames of reference and meaning, beneath the shifting divisions and vicissitudes of our actual history" (Hall, 1990, p.223). That is to say, identity here is produced through the retelling of history, regardless of the interference of other utterances. It can be secured through the memory of a common tradition and history, just like the old medicine man Ku'oosh's healing through ceremony to bring back all the fragmented memories of Tayo to let him reconnect with the Laguna tradition and history. It is not just buried in the past once you lost it with no access to it ever. However, there's coherence with the past and once the connections are rebuilt, the "loss of identity" will begin to heal. In *Ceremony*, Tayo reconnects the relationship with the history in Laguna and regains his lost identity as a Native American through the building of connections by storytelling. As this book has mentioned previously, it is improper to thetically deny this kind of fixed identity because it may function at some certain points. The first ceremony carried out for Tayo is based on the representing of first positioning of Hall. Ku'oosh gives Tayo a scalp ceremony to let him regain his past:

> The way
> I heard it
> was
> in the old days
> long time ago
> they had this
> Scalp Society
> for warriors
> who killed
> or touched
> dead enemies.
>
> They had things
> they must do
> otherwise
> K'oo'ko would haunt their dreams
> with her great fangs and
> everything would be endangered.
> Maybe the rain wouldn't come
> or the deer would go away.

That's why
They had things
They must do

The flute and dancing
blue cornmeal and
hair-washing.

All these things
they had to do. (Silko, 1986, pp.37-38)

The scalp ceremony, connects Tayo as a part of the integrated Laguna history, not just individually separated from it, and the lost identity can only be secured by setting himself in the context of the Native American traditional culture. But according to old Ku'oosh, the scalp ceremony is so traditional for nowadays that he is not sure that whether it can cure Tayo's sickness. It turns out that Tayo is getting better after Ku'oosh's treatment:

> He could eat regular food. He seldom vomited any more. Some nights he even slept all night without dreams. (Silko, 1986, p.39)

So, once Tayo reconnects with the Laguna tradition, he consoles himself with the coherence that is discovered through ceremony. Conforming to the traditional culture temporally saves the protagonist from sickness. He identifies himself as part of the traditional Indian culture and comforts himself in the Laguna history. However, as Ku'oosh tells Tayo, things are different now, and counting alone on the traditional therapy is not enough anymore. There are people who had the scalp ceremony but still not get better. "There are some things we can't cure like we used to, not since the white people came" (Silko, 1986, p.38). In other words, just counting on the tradition can no longer suit in the current society since the cultural context has changed greatly. Like it is described, "the old man would not have believed white warfare — killing across great distances without knowing who or how many had died. It is all too alien to comprehend ... even if he could have led him through the fallen jungle trees and muddy caters of torn earth to show him the dead, the old man would not have believed anything so monstrous" (Silko, 1986, p.36). So, Ku'oosh's ceremony is positioned in the old times, it is fixed without any changes from the society, and it needs to take in something new to survive. The ceremony is not finished, it needs further elements to be complete.

So, the above analysis reaches an opinion that only positioning in the fixed culture of the past cannot solve the problem in current society that is filled with so many differences. To put it simple, the solution for it is to accept the diversity by adding in with the newness and difference based on the tradition and similarity. This is the second positioning of Hall's idea on cultural identity:

> This second position recognizes that, as well as the many points of similarity, there are also critical points of deep and significant *difference* which constitute "what we really are;" or rather — since history has intervened — "what we have become." We cannot speak for very long, with any exactness, about "one experience, one identity," without acknowledging its other side — the ruptures and discontinuities. Cultural identity, in this second sense, is a matter of "becoming" as well as of "being." It belongs to the future as much as to the past. It is not something which already exists, transcending place, time, history, and culture. Cultural identities come from somewhere, have histories. But like everything which is historical, they undergo constant transformation. (1990, p.225)

In other words, the identity construction is a dynamic transforming process that requires cultural difference as well as cultural similarity and continuity. The cultural identity is not some "transcendental spirit" that a group of people hold which history has no influence on, and "it is not a fixed origin to which we can make some final and absolute return" (Hall, 1990, p. 226). So, even if we might secure some certain identities once in some positions in history, the ancestry spirit is not something we can count on forever when difference breaks in because history is always developing in a continuous way. The proper attitude that one should hold towards the problem of cultural conflicts is to accept and take advantage of the difference through a simultaneous interaction of similarity and difference①.

As for the novel *Ceremony*, the background is set in exactly the same cultural context where the protagonist, Tayo is himself a hybrid of Native Indian and the white, and he is suffering from the conflicts of both cultures. Feeling uncertain of his identity, he turns to another medicine man Betonie for help. Different from the old Ku'oosh, he is a

① The author has stated in previous chapter that similarity is the common cultural experience or some fixed essential spirit from history. Difference is something new and peculiar that breaks in due to separations. Similarity signifies continuity with the past and difference signifies discontinuity. Similarity and difference will not exist independently. Cultural identity is formed through admitting and accepting the discontinuity on the basis of a common ground.

hybrid of Indian and Mexican:

> He looked at his face. The cheekbones were like the wings of a hawk soaring away from his board nose; he wore a drooping thick mustache; the hairs were steel grey. Then Tayo looked at his eyes. They were hazel like his own. (Silko, 1986, p.119)

Betonie's hybrid identity has already indicated that Tayo's second ceremony will be quite different and consists of some new and changeable elements. Usually, people don't prefer changes, they choose to live in their comfort zone, which is the result of unbroken colonial discourse. However, since the white come, the society has changed greatly, the medicine man Betonie's household goods signify that the improved type of ceremony will combine multiple elements of different cultures. There are not only "woolly brown goatskin," "dried sage and the brown leaves of mountain tobacco" which represent the style of Indian tradition, but also "bundles of newspaper," "piles of telephone books," "green glass of the Coke bottles" and "layers of old calendars" which are placed in the same room of Betonie, and represent the influence of the white culture. This is the blending thought that old Betonie holds towards the colliding of different cultures. That he emphasizes the importance of transformation is also embodied in his attitude towards ceremony:

> In many ways, the ceremonies have always been changing ... At one time, the ceremonies as they had been performed were enough for the way the world was then. But after the white people came, elements in this world began to shift; and it became necessary to create new ceremonies. I have made changes in the rituals. The people mistrust this greatly, but only this growth keeps the ceremonies strong. (Silko, 1986, p.126)

So, the ceremony that Betonie is going to perform on Tayo is the "revised" version which gets its power from the white as well as the traditional Indian since "it is the only way." "It cannot be done alone. We must have power from everywhere. Even the power we can get from the whites." Based on the multi-cultural consciousness, Betonie develops the ceremony of chant by adding in the new elements in current society besides the traditional contents. He makes the sand painting of rainbows, mountains, and the helper works out the bear footprints. "They guided his feet into the bear footprints" to experience the power and harmony of the universe. When

Tayo wakes up in the dream, he feels:

> There were no boundaries, the world below and the sand paintings inside became the same that night. The mountains from all directions had been gathered there that night. (Silko, 1986, p.145)

Through the ceremony performed by Betonie, Tayo secured his identity and the balance from both the Indian traditional culture and the white culture. He is no longer confined in the Laguna tradition or afraid of the white society. Instead, he sees the possibility of two cultures coexisting and blending. Tayo begins to try to get used to and accept the changing world since one cannot merely depend on the position in the past and tradition. Imagine the human culture as a linear process, and there are different positions on the line; then the construction of identity is the connection and combination of some certain positions that is always in its process of changing and renewal.

Betonie also tells Tayo a story of the witchery on the white to help him see through the white mythology and confront the white society with confidence and power. He explains to Tayo that:

> That is the trickery of the witchcraft ... They want us to believe all evil resides with white people. Then we will look no further to see what is really happening. They want us to separate ourselves from white people, to be ignorant and helpless as we watch our own destruction. But white people are only tools that the witchery manipulates; and I tell you, we can deal with white people, with their machines and their beliefs. We can because we invented white people; it was Indian witchery that made white people in the first place. (Silko, 1986, p.132)

In other words, all the fear or prejudice towards the white from the old times Native American who are not willing to face and accept the changes of the outside world are results of the witchcraft. The trickery on the white is actually invented by the old tradition to prevent the new generation from learning and integrating into the white culture because they are afraid of the white society. This is the traditional way Indians choose to fight against the cultural colonization and assimilation of the white. Betonie's story shows a more direct way for Tayo to understand the fact that the world is changing and he should fear no more to accept the transformation and comfort himself in both cultures of

Native Americans and the white. That is the purpose of Betonie's renewed ceremony — to break the boundaries that restricted and confined people in the old tradition and embrace the world with the dynamic transforming process it undergoes.

> The dry skinl
> was still stuck
> to his body.
> But the effects
> of the witchery
> of the evil thing
> began to leave
> his body.
> The effects of the witchery
> of the evil thing
> in his surroundings
> began to turn away.
> It had gone a great distance
> It had gone below the North. (Silko, 1986, p.153)

Tayo is then, under the guidance of Betonie, gradually getting rid of the control of the witchery which this book considers as the psychological colonization of the unprivileged in society. Either the Native American culture or the white culture is basically speaking constructed discourses. So both treatment by old Ku'oosh and Betonie will not completely cure Tayo's sickness and in the end Betonie tells Tayo "the ceremony isn't finished yet":

> One night or nine nights won't do it any more," ... He was drawing in the dirt with his finger. "Remember these stars," he said. "I've seen them and I've seen the spotted cattle; I've seen a mountain and I've seen a woman. (Silko, 1986, p.152)

He leads Tayo to find the woman Ts'eh because the treatment here with Betonie is done. There's nothing more Betonie can provide to let Tayo get better, and he still need further inspiration to complete the ceremony and get recovered, which this book deems is to demystify and decolonize the authoritative discourse that he is performing. Searching for the stars, spotted cattle and the woman Ts'eh is to guide Tayo to regain his power from nature and the genuine self.

In general, this section mainly explains the protagonist's attempt for identity comfort in early stages of the novel *Ceremony* and he eventually locates himself in a dynamic transforming cultural process. He identifies himself in the changing society as well as the Indian tradition. Depending alone on either one cannot succeed in the diaspora situation of cultural default in current Native American reservation; and there are some other characters who can illustrate this problem.

To begin with, the white society has showed the Native American with great attraction, the modernism and freedom that Indians have never expected or experienced before, and the elegance and superiority the white asserted. For those returning soldiers, holding the illusion with them that they are once accepted and respected by the white society during the war, they are eager to integrate into the white culture. And Rocky, representing the young generation of Laguna, is the pride of Auntie because he behaves just like the white. However, Rocky is just the result of white colonization and assimilation, and he is only blindly performing what the white enforced on him and believe in everything the colonizer teaches him without hesitation:

> "Those books are written by scientists. They know everything there is to know about beef cattle. That's the trouble with the way the people around here have always done

> things — they never knew what they were doing." He went back to reading his book. He did not hesitate to speak like that, to his father and his uncle, because the subject was books and scientific knowledge — those things that Rocky had learned to believe in. (Silko, 1986, p.76)

This is the result of cultural colonization that manipulated by the discourse of the white because "they were just educated only enough to know they wanted to leave the reservation." The purpose of cultural assimilation is to use the cultural discourse to manipulate and take advantage of the Native Americans without accepting them as part of the white society. So conforming oneself to the white culture is by no means the solution for the Native American.

Other Indians, firmly entrenched in the doctrines of traditional Indian culture, are unwilling to come in to contact with the white culture. They only believe in the common ancestry spirit they hold and take everything else as evil and bad. In fact, they are also colonized by discourse, not of the white, but of the old tradition. And the reason for them to reject and exclude Tayo actually lies in that they are afraid of changes. Tayo's half-breed identity signifies his difference and changes from other Native Indians:

> They are afraid, Tayo. They feel something happening, they can see something happening around them, and it scares them. Indians or Mexicans or whites — most people are afraid of change. (Silko, 1986, pp.99-100)

Cling to history and tradition alone without any changes will also fail in the self-realization of Native American since the world is in itself dynamic. As the old man Ku'oosh's ceremony is unable to heal Tayo, he turns to another medicine man Betonie for help to complete the ceremony. And this is the third self-identification status of Tayo.

The last and the proper self-identification of Tayo is provided by Betonie with a more hybrid status of cultural identity. It is based on the recognition of both Native American culture and the white culture. And this hybridity acknowledges the similarity as well as the difference. Just like Tayo's mixed-blood identity, the attitude one should hold towards the colliding of different cultures is formed through the changing contexts. The proper Native American identity for them to conform is built through the dynamic transforming process with different history and culture constantly intervening, on a basis of the common ground of the traditional Indian culture, excluding neither the tradition nor the newness. This is the new Native American identity in the changing world.

However, according to Betonie, even by conforming to the changing identity, Tayo still needs further ceremony to recover. This is why this book previously claimed that Hall's idea on diaspora identity cannot successfully contribute to the diaspora experience since it depends on the essentialism of the concept of identity. As far as this book is concerned, identity itself is a concept of essence and mythology, so the idea of searching and performing certain identity is by no means the proper solution for diasporic subjects to succeed in their diaspora experience. It will only lead to the status of being colonized by given discourses.

3. Conclusion

Comprehending the protagonist Tayo's self-identification by performing different positionings of cultures, we can better understand his diasporic experience in Leslie Marmon Silko's *Ceremony*. There should be no such concept as pre-existing or pre-given identity that is internal and essential for diasporic groups. It is just the naturalization of repetitive performance of social discourse that acts on them again and again to let them believe it is real, authentic and pre-existing. Thus, diaspora identity is just the outcome of continuous performing of certain discourse, which is compulsory and violently enforced by cultural authority on diasporic subjects. That is to say, diasporic groups will never get rid of the control of given discourses if they keep searching and performing the identity constructed for them. Tayo and other veterans constantly pursue for the white culture which they believe has been existed there all the time as real and authentic for them to perform. As for Tayo, he is also trapped in the myth of fixed identity and cannot get rid of it. After realizing the fact that they are not accepted by the white society, unlike those veterans who find nowhere to fit themselves in, he gradually abandons the identification of white culture and seeks for other possibilities in the Laguna tradition. So the factor to explain the diasporic experience in the first half of this novel as unsuccessful lies in that Tayo never thinks of breaking the social discourses or culture myth; instead, he is always searching and adjusting himself to perform pre-existing or pre-given identities. The problem is that the consciousness of diasporic subjects, like the minority and unprivileged groups in hostland denies the subjects' sovereignty and stresses their performativity. So, they are easily controlled by the given discourses, and the repetitive performances of certain discourses which are deemed as their identities add to the naturalization of diaspora identities. Tayo is trapped in this kind of endless circle of performances. Diasporic subject should not be subject to some pre-given identity that authoritative discourses violently enforced. Actually, there should be no concept as identity for diasporas to follow. Diasporas are diaspora as a result of their performances, not because the pre-existing identity claimed them to be diasporas. So this book believes that a successful diaspora experience will not be trapped in searching for some identity essence and confining to it, which may lead to a gloomy situation for diasporic groups to deal with.

Ⅴ. *Ceremony*: Decolonization of Given Discourses and Ecological Reconstruction

Searching and conforming to given identities will never secure diasporic groups from the cultural dilemma. To break the colonial discourses and get rid of the enforced identity is a more proper attempt in pursuing diaspora identity. In this chapter, the focus is to analyze the related question with the latter half of *Ceremony* to work out a solution for the problem of diaspora and diaspora identity. This chapter will discuss the diaspora experience of the protagonist Tayo to prove it as a positive and successful example to provide diasporic groups with possibilities to get rid of colonial discourse and gain power from another context.

This chapter examines how Tayo extricates himself from colonial discourse and the given identities. As this book has mentioned above, Tayo's ceremony with Betonie is not finished yet. To complete his ceremony, he then met Ts'eh, the important female character in *Ceremony* who leads Tayo to fulfill his ceremony and get recovered from the sickness. That Tayo rebuilds the balance and reconnects with nature through the guidance of Ts'eh endows himself with inner and genuine power of human being. As far as this book is concerned, Tayo's recovery lies in the disillusionment of culture and identity myth. It is based on the decolonization of certain discourse and de-essentialization of pre-given identity. As Bhabha argued that culture should never be considered as fixed or stabilized, instead, it is fluid and constructed through discourses. Depending on Butler's theory of Performativity, this book reckons that diasporic subjects should get rid of the situation of repetitive and continuous performance of enforced discourses. For Tayo, his completion of ceremony and success of self-recovery is the process of deconstruction of given identity. However, decolonization or deconstruction is not the only purpose; self-recovery or self-realization is. Since discourse is broken, and pre-given or fixed identity then is no longer available, what will the pre-existing context or discourse be for him to perform? So, Tayo takes his power not from the cultural or political context, but from other contexts, namely nature, land, and some other fundamental elements of human beings. That's what he performs and where he gets the genuine power to complete himself.

1. Decolonization of Colonial Discourses

But the effects
of the witchery
of the evil thing
began to leave
his body.
The effects of the witchery
of the evil thing
in his surroundings
began to turn away. (Silko, 1986, p.153)

To complete the ceremony, as this book said before, Tayo needs to demystify the cultural illusion or decolonize the colonial discourse. Merely depending on the identification of certain culture will definitely lead to the repetitive performance of given discourses that traps and manipulates the unprivileged. According to Bhabha, all the deemed cultural essences are constructed discourses given by the social authority[①]. Then conforming to certain culture is in fact being colonized by social discourses. "The ideological function of colonialist discourse serves to continue the paradigm of the native as Other," and "the underlying purpose serves to bolster the political aims of the colonialists" (Bird, 2005, p.96). Only by decolonization can the unprivileged negotiate in the postcolonial discourse. However, the colonial authoritative discourse gets contradictions in itself that will eventually lead to the deconstruction of it, and this is what Bhabha noted as the ambivalent status of cultural difference.

Ambivalence here in Bhabha's case bears a special connotation to refer to the complicated relations or status between the colonizer and the colonized. He argued that the interrelationship between the colonizer and the colonized should not be completely contradicted or opposed. The colonizer was not absolutely authoritative and the colonized was not entirely passive. This is the status of ambivalence; through constant negotiation and communication, the possibilities of resistance might occur. Similar to the strategy of "mimicry," it is

---

① See the third chapter.

initially carried out by the colonizer who aims to manipulate the colonized by letting them mimic their extrinsic appearance, action or behavior as well as the inherent culture or values.

The status of ambivalence is not favored by the colonizer since it may get contradicted in itself, which will break in the continuity and authority of the colonization. The purpose of the colonizer is to produce the colonized group as mimics that are subordinate or subject to their colonial discourses. Thus to meet their colonizing ambition. Mimicry is the same case. The aim of mimicry is to educate and moralize the colonized by compulsorily enforcing colonial discourses on them. But in Bhabha's view, the strategy of mimicry is also filled with contradictions. On the one hand, the colonizer trys to civilize the colonized by providing them with access to the elegant and superior western culture. On the other hand, they always keep reminding the colonized of their inferiority and barbarity by ontology to resist and deny their civilization. It is exactly the difference of the colonizer / superior and colonized / inferior they want to maintain that leads to the collapse of colonial discourses. This is why Bhabha deems that the colonial discourse cannot succeed, and decolonization will provide the unprivileged and minority with possibilities to open up new spaces for them to negotiate in.

In the novel of *Ceremony*, the protagonist Tayo, at the beginning of his treatment, has been searching for his cultural identity, which is in fact being colonized by the authoritative discourse. His sickness seems to be caused by the loss of identity; however, it is never the root of the problem. So, gaining himself different identities still cannot complete his ceremony and get him recovered. The solution for it is not to count on the pre-given identity which will lead to the repetitive and cyclic performance, but to demystify and decolonize the cultural illusion.

As analyzed above, Tayo begins to realize the importance and necessity for him to decolonize the given discourse rather than searching and performing certain identities. After Betonie's ceremony, he feels the witchery begins to leave his body, and the effect of evil thing is also turning away. The witchery here mentioned in Betonie's words carries specific functions:

> Witchery works to scare people, to make them fear growth. But it has always been necessary, and more than ever now, it is. Otherwise we won't make it. We won't survive. That's what

> the witchery is counting on: that we will cling to the ceremonies the way they were, and then their power will triumph, and the people will be no more. (Silko, 1986, p.126)

In other words, witchery is like a control form that makes people perform and act as it requires. And that's why this book claims the witchery in Betonie's words is like what we define as colonial discourse. It exists to speak for the authority and enforce certain discourses on the inferior in society to manipulate them as they needed. So if Tayo merely counts on the traditional ceremony or some fixed identities, it just satisfies the authority's intention of cultural colonization. Tayo's brother Rocky is the case, as he is colonized by the white cultural discourse. As this book previously discussed, he is the representative of people who completely abandon the tradition and conform to the white culture. He shows disrespect to his father and uncle, Robert and Josiah, when talking about the cattle business "because the subject was books and scientific knowledge — those things that Rocky had learned to believe in." That he believes in everything he is taught and educated is the result of psychological colonization. Then it will be the triumph of colonial discourse towards the colonized. However, if Rocky is educated to be both extrinsically and intrinsically the same with the white, as Auntie wishes "becoming what she had always wanted: someone who could not only make sense of the outside world but become part of it," the colonizer will lose its position of superiority, which is definitely unacceptable for them. So on the one hand, the colonizers want to keep the differences between the colonized and them; on the other hand, they aim to assimilate the colonized with their culture to control them. As a result, it is inevitable to meet the contradictions in itself, which will in turn lead to the collapse of colonial discourse.

Tayo, after the two ceremonies with old Ku'oosh and Betonie, finally begins to see through the illusion of culture. In order to gain himself power from other context rather than culture, he needs first to get away from the witchery to decolonize the given discourse. "It is a departure from and unmasking of the constructs that have draped us since the colonization of this continent" (Bird, 2005, p.95). Betonie has enlightened him with the witchery story to let him understand that the deemed and pre-existing culture is constructed discourse of the social authority. So it happens to Tayo after he leaves Betonie that he is "holding his heaving belly, trying to vomit out everything — all the past, all his life" since he has been confined in the illusion of given and enforced discourses during his past. Leaving the unavailable past behind is the necessary step to a new stage, and "there were transitions that had to be made in order to become whole again, in order to be the people our Mother would remember; transitions, like the boy walking in bear country being called back softly"(Silko, 1986, p.170). Tayo is now turning to the transition of gradually getting rid of the colonization of colonial discourse and rebuilding the self.

With the guidance of old Betonie, Tayo sets out for the speckled cattle. He finds their tracks on the white man Floyd Lee's land, but he would never believe that the cattle are stolen since they are on a white man's ranch. All he could think up is that Floyd Lee is probably buying these cattle from real thieves. So "why did he hesitate to accuse a white man of stealing but not a Mexican or an Indian?" This chapter would reckon that Tayo also finds out that it is the result of psychological colonization which aims to fill the heart of the colonized with lies:

> The lie which they had wanted him to learn: only brown-skinned people were thieves; white people didn't steal,

> because they always had the money to buy whatever they wanted.
>
> The lie. He cut into the wire as if cutting away at the lie inside himself. The liars had fooled everyone, white people and Indians alike; as long as people believed the lies, they would never be able to see what had been done to them or what they were doing to each other ... If the white people never looked beyond the lie, to see that theirs was a nation built on stolen land, then they would never be able to understand how they had been used by the witchery. (Silko, 1986, p.191)

That is how the colonial discourse works: it produces some pre-existing essence to educate the unprivileged and let them believe it is real and authentic that they are born to be. So the unprivileged would live with the lie and engrave in their heart and blood to follow the principle or doctrine. For Tayo, he is gradually getting clear of the illusion and mythology of given discourses. To decolonize it, Tayo presumes that not only the Indians but the white are also victims of colonial discourse. Brown-skinned people are considered as inferior and barbaric while the white as superior and civilized; only the brown-skinned steal while the white never do that. He cuts the wire as if he is cutting the lie, or this chapter would say he is trying to break the colonization of given discourses. By now, Tayo fully understand that it is not the people of brown-skinned or white are responsible for their behavior of suppressed or aggressive, and they should not be blamed for the colonial situation. It is the authoritative discourse and those who stand behind it that are manipulating everything since "the witchery would work so that the people would be fooled into blaming only the whites and not the witchery." And this is the true colonial situation in Tayo's understanding.

Tayo's progress of the next stage of ceremony is carried out with the female character Ts'eh in searching for the speckled cattle. And he is getting his power little by little in this process.

> He had been so intent on finding the cattle that he had forgotten all the events of the past days and past years. Hunting the cattle was good for that. Old Betonie was right. It was a cure for that, and maybe for other things too. The spotted cattle wouldn't be lost any more, scattered through his dreams, driven by his hesitation to admit they had been stolen, that the land — all of it — had been stolen from them. (Silko, 1986, p.192)

That is to say, following Betonie's guidance to find the spotted cattle is also a progress of gaining himself power and healing his sickness, and the "cure" here is actually the disillusionment of mythologies of discourses. Once the cattle are found, they wouldn't lost or in other words, the truth will not be covered or mystified any longer when given discourses are decolonized. It will open up new cultural spaces beyond the boundaries of tradition and the white. "They would leave the questions of lineage, clan, and family name to the people in the village"(Silko, 1986, p.223). That the half-breed identity of Tayo is no longer troubling him. Those people care about and despise his mix-blood because they consider his other half of white lineage as evil and disgraceful under the old witchery. All those colonial discourses for Tayo have collapsed by now. So if the cultural context cannot provide Tayo with strength, where should he gain his power and get recovered?

This chapter would explore that the strength of healing and recovery for the protagonist in *Ceremony* is mainly acquired from two aspects that are respectively nature and love. Ts'sh has led him to a ceremony to ignore the influence of culture and feel the relationship of human and nature. The

Indian people have been warned that "the balance of the world had been disturbed and the people could expect droughts and harder days to come" (Silko, 1986, p.186) ever since the white's invasion. So maybe the element of nature will be a crucial element in the balancing of himself as well as the changing society①.

> Sunrise!
> We come at sunrise
> to greet you.
> We call you
> at sunrise.
> Father of the clouds
> you are beautiful
> at sunrise.
> Sunrise! (Silko, 1986, p.182)

Sunrise here in this novel is illustrated as the source of the strength and power for Tayo to regain. He is getting the feeling that "the instant of the dawn was an event which in a single moment gathered all things together — the last stars, the mountaintops, the clouds, and the winds" (Silko,

---

① There are a lot of nature elements that have been described in *Ceremony*. This chapter will only list one at this point; others will be discussed separately later.

1986, p.182). Everything is lighted and filled with strength in one sunbeam, which later has helped him to gain confidence in overcoming the fear and uncertainties in dealing with Emo and others:

> At that moment in the sunrise, it was all so beautiful, everything, from all directions, evenly, perfectly, balancing day with night, summer months with winter. The valley was enclosing this totality, like mind holding all thoughts together in a single moment.
>
> "The strength came from here, from this feeling. It had always been there. He stood there with the sun on his face, and he thought maybe he might make it after all". (Silko, 1986, p.237)

So Tayo is now acquiring the strength and confidence of conquering the threatening of Emo and his accomplice. He believes that with the power gained from the sun, he will finally make it. In his eyes, he sees that the power of sun combines and balances everything, day and night, summer and winter, and that every single element can be integrated into one. It is similar to the human thoughts in that once different recognitions and values confront with each other, rather than contradictions irreconcilable, the natural strength of nature will hold them together. Like Tayo's half-breed identity, it should not be discriminated against. On the contrary, the balancing status might contain greater strength and possibilities. That the nature can balance contradictions and oppositions into an integrated and harmonious one has enlightened Tayo of his mix-blood heritage. The sunbeam as well spills over Tayo's body and mind to strengthen him with the determination to balance the conflicts inside. That he feels the strength to defeat Emo is the access to a balanced status of tradition and the white within himself. So the power endowed by the nature helps Tayo to overcome the witchery on Emo and others. Tayo is representing a new style of Native Americans who are no longer the slave or product of colonial discourse. He is powerful, harmonious and peaceful, and he can conquer the problem and confusion of cultural and identity default, which is also the situation of diasporas.

Another aspect this chapter would like to mention to contribute to the recovery of Tayo is "the love he felt from her" after he meets the woman Ts'eh. He begins to understand that what is always supporting and strengthening him is not the commonly deemed culture. Instead, it is the love inside and surrounding him that helps him to make through all the difficulties and sufferings encountered in the process of recovery.

> The mountain outdistanced their destruction, just as love had outdistanced death. The mountain could not be lost to them, because it was in their bones; Josiah and Rocky were not far away. They were close; they had always been close. And he loved them then as he had always loved them, the feeling pulsing over him as strong as it had ever been. They love him that way; he could still feel the love they had for him. The damage that had been done had never reached this feeling ... and nothing was ever lost as long as the love remained. (Silko, 1986, pp.219-220)

So for Tayo, he is no longer fascinated with and manipulated by certain discourses that he once pursued for and conformed to because it is artificially constructed and violently enforced on the unprivileged like Tayo. As a result, it can never transcend the power of nature and love, which is strong, changing, transformative and everlasting. The effect or result of constructed discourse might function for a while. However, it is fixed, illusionary and periodical, so it stands a good chance of being decolonized or demystified. Aware of the uncertainty and constructiveness of pre-existing culture, Tayo feels the love he possesses from everywhere that has always been there with him and should be the source of his belief. He will fear no more and lose no more; he is holding love with him to save himself as well as others. With all those elements, the transition is completed.

> Hummingbird and Fly thanked him.
> They took the tobacco to old Buzzard.
> "Here it is. We finally got it but it
> sure wasn't very easy."
> "Okay," Buzzard said
> "Go back and tell them
> I'll purify the town."
>
> And he did —
> first to the east
> then to the south
> then to the west
> and finally to the north.
> Everything was set straight again
> after all that ck'o'yo' magic.

The storm clouds returned
the grass and plants started growing again.
There was food
and the people were happy again.
So she told them
Stay out of trouble
from now on.

It isn't very easy
to fix up things again.
Remember that
next time
some ck'o'yo magician
comes to town. (Silko, 1986, pp.255-256)

So nature is the cure for everything. When Tayo no longer relies on the cultural context to regain his power and reconstruct his identity, he finds the influence of nature. He clings and submits to the nature to gain his power. Like the hummingbird and fly, he visits Rio Puerco Valley, Mount Taylor, Acoma and mesas to complete his transition. Tayo has finished his ceremony and recovered. Meanwhile he also finds the cure for all the Native Americans. After he returns to Laguna, representing the new Laguna spirit, everything is reaching to a harmonious status, including the conflicts between the native and the white, his disgraceful origins, even Auntie's prejudice. So Laguna is itself always transformative, and disillusionment and decolonization of the given discourse is the way to rebirth.

The protagonist's recovery depends on the context of nature rather than culture, which this chapter would like to explore with Deep Ecology in the following section.

2. Ecological Self-realization

As this book has suggested before that when Tayo gets rid of the illusion and colonization of given discourse, he no longer chooses to gain his power from the cultural context. Instead, he finds balance and strengths in the process of exploring nature under Ts'eh's guidance and gets cured through a status of Self-realization in negotiating with nature. Tayo recognizes himself from the interrelations of every existing natural element and reaches the ultimate recovery when it comes to the realization of ecological holism, which coincides with what Arne Naess initially puts forward as the idea of Deep Ecology. Different from the anthropocentrism of shallow ecology①, deep ecology is of ecocentrism that takes the nature and human beings as a whole. Everything is interdependent and human being is just a part of it under the view of ecological holism. The survival of all beings depends on the wholeness of the ecological system, not the other way around②.

Deep ecology, which aims to seek for the true value of mankind and to propose a harmonious lifestyle and rational social construction, suggests two ultimate norms as the fundamental principles, namely Self-realization and ecocentric equalitarianism. Ecocentric equalitarianism claims that everything is just a part of the ecosphere interdependent on each other, which shares the equal rights to survive and develop to realize its intrinsic value. The equality here refers to a real and inherent equal status by their intrinsic value, and there's no hierarchical level and distinction between human beings and other creatures in the ecosphere. Mankind

---

① Shallow ecology only concentrates on the well-being of mankind and its ultimate goal for protecting environment and resources is that all beings can live a better life. So the profit of mankind is the first consideration.

② It refers to the opinion of shallow ecology that it is human being who will take control of everything, including the survival of nature. The existing of natural world is to serve the needs of mankind who live separately from nature and take advantage of nature.

should never consider themselves as superior and advantageous compared with others. Meanwhile the other norm of Self-realization is what this book prefers to borrow from Naess to illustrate Tayo's recovery that "goes beyond the modern Western *self* which is defined as an isolated ego striving primarily for hedonistic gratification or for a narrow sense of individual salvation in this life or the next." So to explain the idea of Self-realization, we need first to define the "Self" in Self-realization.

"Self" here in capital letter is different from what we usually deemed as the self in social sense. Naess argues that there are three stages for self-identification, from ego to self, then finally the Ecological Self, which is realized through the symbiosis of mankind and the nature. As Naess noted:

> The ecosophical outlook is developed through an identification so deep that one's *own self* is no longer adequately delimited by the personal ego or the organism. One experiences oneself to be a genuine part of all life. Each living being is understood as a goal in itself, *in principle* on an equal footing with one's own ego. (1990, p.174)

Ego, self and Self is philosophically the deep, comprehensive and ecological self separately. The three stages of self-realization are processes for mankind to expand the identification that all beings should be treated as one inseparable part from the ecosphere, and nobody can get self-realized alone and individually. The capitalized Self will only be secured when you treat yourself as part of the ecosphere. And when a man reaches the status of Ecological Self, he will find and identify himself in the interaction and realization of the natural world. This is the Self-realization of deep ecology norm that only the realization of the organic wholeness can bring the realization of man.

> This process of the full unfolding of the self can also be summarized by the phrase, 'No one is saved until we are all saved,' where the phrase "one" includes not only me, an individual human, but all humans, whales, grizzly bears, whole rain forest ecosystems, mountains and rivers, the tiniest microbes in the soil, and so on. (Devall & Sessions, 1985, p.67)

Or as Naess explained "Self-realization" as the one ultimate norm of Ecosophy T,

> I do not use this expression in any narrow, individualistic sense. I want to give it an expanded meaning based on the distinction between a large comprehensive Self and narrow

> egoistic self as conceived of in certain Eastern traditions of *atman*. This large comprehensive Self (with a capital "S") embraces all the life forms on the planet (and elsewhere?) together with their individual selves (jivas). If I were to express this ultimate norm in a few words, I would say: "Maximize (long-range, universal) Self-realization! (Naess, 1995, p.80)

The author would put it this way concerning this book's argument. If one wants to identify and realize oneself, it is not simply the realization of *self* who is existing as an individual in society or living separately from the ecosphere. This kind of realization is still constrained in the aspect and context of social and culture, which will improbably be free from the colonization and illusion of given discourse. However, the colonial discourse will restrain people from gaining power and realizing the *self*. Moreover, this social self is in fact an violently enforced and given illusion that social authority constructed. Consequently, as the unprivileged, they should turn to the ecological self to regain their power and reach the status of Self-realization since nature will endow them with intrinsic strength and value. Feeling the balance and equality of the nonhuman world and identifying with the organic wholeness of the ecosystem, the completion of all the life forms will eventually bring the Self-realization and identification of mankind in the sense of deep ecology.

As for the protagonist Tayo in *Ceremony*, the recovery and healing of his sickness is secured only when he reaches the Ecological Self in the realization through the interactive and interdependent relationship among the ecosphere. His success lies in that he goes beyond the narrow and conservative social self or ego, which is to some extent the product and result of some given or certain discourses. So, after the decolonization and disillusionment of constructed discourses, Tayo is neither adhering to the Native American culture nor conforming to the white culture. And according to the norms of deep ecology, he just goes beyond the cultural context and realized the Self in the organic wholeness of all living forms. As Bill Devall and George Sessions once stated:

> But the deep ecology sense of self requires a further maturity and growth, an identification which goes beyond humanity to include the nonhuman world. We must see beyond our narrow contemporary cultural assumptions and values, and the conventional wisdom of our time and place, and this is the best

achieved by the meditative deep questioning process. Only in this way can we hope to attain full mature personhood and uniqueness. (1985, p.67)

In other words, in deep ecology, the ultimate goal of self-realization is no longer constrained in the domain of human being. Moreover, it covers the sphere of nonhuman world. And cultural context is not the only source for people to gain their self identification since it will lead to the cyclic repetition of psychological colonization and identity performances. To get rid of this immature or social self, one should seek to achieve the ecological Self in the process of a whole and integrated standpoint to discover the truth. Thus let's turn to the experience of Tayo to check the recovery through Self-realization.

In the novel *Ceremony*, natural elements have always been described and applied in narrating the protagonist's healing and recovery process, from the mountain, river, canyon, forest, sun, to lion, snake, bear, cattle, even tiny creatures like bumblebee and fly, etc. All these are part of the whole ecosystem like human beings are, which cannot exist and live independently. Just as Naess explained the Self-realization norm of deep ecology: "Live and let live," represents a biocentric and holistic point of view that asks people to go beyond the context of culture and position oneself in a larger vision of Self. And this is also the reason for Tayo to achieve his recovery against the sickness. Like Tayo once remembered that Josiah had talked to him about the importance of nature:

> He pointed his chin at the springs and around at the narrow canyon. "This is where we come from, see. This sand, this stone, these trees, the vines, all the windflowers. This earth keeps us going." He took off his hat and wiped his forehead on his shirt. "These dry years you hear some people complaining, you know, about the dust and the wind, and how dry it is. But the wind and the dust, they are part of life too, like the sun and the sky. You don't swear at them. It's people, see. They're the ones. The old people used to say that droughts happen when people forget, when people misbehave." (Silko, 1986, pp.45-46)

According to Josiah, nature is the source of power and strength for human beings to survive, and it is also a kind of living forms just like mankind belongs to the ecosystem. Both human beings and nature are equally existing and independently affected. And since all beings are components of the whole ecosphere and cannot be talked about separately, it is consequently that the recovery of nature in *Ceremony* will bring the recovery of individual like Tayo. Also it is inevitable that Tayo can regain his power from every single element in nature when he gets rid of the colonization of social discourses in cultural context because he sees and finds himself in nature. He realizes the Self in nature beyond the boundaries of culture, convention or any values he once conforms to.

What we have discussed above about the organic wholeness of ecosystem is from the space dimension of mankind, nature or other forms of living creature. Besides this, this chapter would like to extend it to the time dimension of past, present and future. In other words, the property of wholeness and continuity can as well lend itself to the issue of human evolution. That the human beings as a whole regardless of nationality, race, color or clan, etc. constitute a long river of human history, in which they share the same origin from the very beginning. We can find the similar description in *Ceremony* when Betonie answered Tayo's puzzlement of seeing Josiah when he was fighting with the Japanese in the jungle in Philippine:

> "The Japanese," the medicine man went on, as though he were trying to remember something. "It isn't surprising you saw him with them. You saw who they were. Thirty thousand years ago they were not strangers. You saw what the evil had done: you saw the witchery ranging as wide as the world." (Silko, 1986, p.124)

In Betonie's view, no matter what the nationality is, whether Native American or Japanese, they all belong to the same origin of mankind as a whole and continuous beings in the time dimension. So it is no surprise that Tayo saw him. The current society of classification or hierarchical order of human being is the result of cultural illusion and psychological colonization which in Betonie's words, is called the witchery. It is the constructed discourse that speaks for the authoritative politics to suppress the minority or unprivileged and leads to the social status of hierarchy, difference and contradiction. So when Tayo frees himself from the control of witchery, he discovers that the difference can only exist on the level of cultural context, and there should be no priority towards any people since they are all part of the human history. So when Tayo sees beyond the cultural construction of time span, he sees a larger world and gains a stronger Self. And this book believes this wholeness and continuity in the time dimension also contribute to the recovery and identification of Tayo.

Back to the question of Self-realization in deep ecology, the process of identification undergoes three different stages of ego, social self and ecological self. And since we have talked about the ecological self-realization of Tayo above, now let's examine the status of social self to acquire the causality and necessity of transition. Actually, the social self can easily be found in the habitual performances of the white:

> but nothing was lost; all was retained between the sky and the earth, and within himself. He had lost nothing. The snow-covered mountain remained, without regard to titles of ownership or the white ranchers who thought they possessed it. They logged the trees, they killed the deer, bear, and mountain lions, they build their fences high; but the mountain was far greater than any or all of these things. (Silko, 1986, p.219)

The white have taken themselves as the master of the nature or the unprivileged group such as Indians. They separate themselves from the ecosphere to take advantage of others, which is the performance of their social self that argues for hierarchical order and priority. However, what they think they may achieve in the conquest and depredation of the nature still outstretches their control because nature will not submit to the construction of culture. Nature is bearing much greater and stronger power that outdistances anything factitious. So it is inevitable that the social self will eventually transit to the ecological Self, or we could say that the social identity is doomed to be disillusioned or demystified in the sense of deep ecology. When identification is secured in the ecological whole, one is realizing the Self unbounded from the *self* or in other words, the psychological colonization.

3. Conclusion

This chapter mainly explores another type of diaspora experience with Leslie Marmon Silko's novel *Ceremony* and analyzes it as a positive and successful example for diasporas to solve their problems of cultural default. This book's argument here extends the previous illustration and comes to the point that decolonization or disillusionment is the way for diasporas to get rid of given discourses, and gaining power from other context rather than culture can avoid the traps of repetitive or habitual identity performances in postcolonial situation. In the novel *Ceremony*, the protagonist Tayo is a half-breed of Native American and the white who attains his identification in neither side. His physical sickness signifies that the contradictions between the cultures of both Native American and the white lead him nowhere to locate himself. However, after several ceremonies with the medicine men Ku'oosh, Betonie and another female character Ts'eh, the protagonist gets recovered through the identification with nature to realize the Self in him. So this chapter would claim that the recovery of Tayo or in other words the success of his diasporic experience lies in two main procedures that are separately decolonization and Self-realization. To make it clearer, diasporas, as the unprivileged or minority in society, are living the life under the colonization of given discourses constructed by the authoritative politics. As long as the illusion exists, they will never get rid of the inferior status in society and acquire their independent cultural identities. So, decolonization or disillusionment is the first step. Nevertheless, when they no longer cling to and perform some given cultures or identities, what should they perform and where could they gain their power and locate themselves? If it is still the cultural context, they would fall into another cycle of psychological colonization and identity performance. Thus, this chapter reckons that diasporas should gain power from other context. In Tayo's case, he reaches the status of Self-realization in the process of identifying himself with nature. He sees himself in nature and gains his power from natural elements to heal his sickness.

The idea of decolonization of discourse mainly comes from Bhabha's theory of postcolonialism. What Betonie told Tayo about the witchery is to some extent similar to the concept of social discourse, and it is the prevailing of witchery leads to the conflicts between the Indian and the white just like that cultural discourses differentiate people with hierarchical orders. When staying out of the constrain of witchery, Tayo no longer feels alienated and estranged as before. So, the decolonization takes him to the first stage of recovery that he is no longer conforming to given identity and constant performance. Only when unbound from those given discourses, can Tayo gain the possibility of realizing himself from nature.

When it finally comes to the last ceremony of the protagonist's healing process, the female character Ts'eh leads him to the stage of searching and identifying himself with natural elements to gain power. Referring to Naess's theory of Deep Ecology, this chapter borrowed his idea of Self-realization to explore the problem of Tayo's recovery. Realizing the Self in the completion of ecological wholeness is the ultimate approach for him to secure his existence, and that's why so many natural elements are described in this novel — they are the sources of his recovery. Besides the concept of Self-realization in space dimension, this chapter also explained Tayo's recovery in the dimension of time. By saying this, this chapter means that there is a possibility that we do not position diasporas in the fixed stereotypes of nationality, race or color, instead, take the whole human race from a time span of evolution as the holism. Regardless of ethnicity, nationality, gender or other elements, the conception of the mankind wholeness is considered as an endless flow of human development. Setting oneself in the time dimension of holism is also a resource for diasporic groups to position themselves and gain their power.

Ⅵ. Conclusion

So far, the study mainly involved the problem of diaspora and diaspora identity and made analyses through the text *Ceremony* to discuss the possibility for diasporic groups to locate themselves in their dispersing experiences. Rather than subject to some pre-given or enforced cultural identity, this book considered getting rid of identity performance, breaking the colonial discourse and gaining power from other context might be a more proper solution for diasporas to succeed in their dispersing experiences.

This book reckoned here that the definition of diaspora should be specified based on the traditional one concentrating on geographical level to the aspect of psychological or mental displacement. In other words, counting on the geographical dislocation alone was insufficient of delimiting a diaspora.

The movements that result in exile, expatriates, immigrants, alien residents, etc. might be easily confused with the category of diasporas. So this book claimed that the crucial element in distinguishing diasporas from others fell to the domain of cultural identity. Thus diasporas here referred to the group of people who were displaced from their original homeland to other places both geographically and mentally but had no myth or illusion in neither homeland nor hostland culture. Then where should they locate themselves spiritually? This led to the problem of diaspora identity.

The issue of diaspora identity by no means shared similar contents with cultural identity. In the first place, diasporic groups did not believe in cultural myth and identify themselves with homeland or hostland culture that were deemed under postmodernism as constructed and pre-given. Secondly, for diasporic groups who belonged to the unprivileged and minority in society, positioning themselves in the cultural context cannot achieve the negotiation with the discourse that were constructed and manipulated by the privileged and authorities. Their spiritual home could only be achieved by interrupting the dualistic oppositions and breaking the psychologically colonizing discourses. So diaspora identity this book argued here would never fall into the same category of cultural identity. It went beyond the domain of cultural context and gained power from somewhere else.

This book elaborated this argument on diaspora identity with Silko's novel *Ceremony* mentioned previously. The first half described an unsuccessful diasporic experience of the protagonist Tayo who kept searching and conforming to some given cultural identities. However, identity was just the result of continuous and repetitive performance of constructed social discourses. In the case of this novel, the protagonist Tayo was performing the given identity that was constructed by the authority and was violently enforced on him without some pre-existing or internal cultural essence. It is the anticipation of essence and repetitive performances that naturalized it. It's aim is to make people believe what they constantly perform as real and pre-existing. Then subject to the concept of cultural identity would easily trap diasporas in the cyclic performing of enforced discourses and they could never position themselves as expected. So searching and conforming to pre-given identity was never the solution for diaspora situation. The analysis with the first half of the novel *Ceremony* supported this argument that subject to given identity would only lead to the failure of diaspora experience.

The latter half of the novel *Ceremony*, on the contrary, provided with a positive result of diaspora experience and the protagonist's recovery and Self-realization with nature gave a vision for the diasporic groups. Tayo at the beginning was performing and subject to certain identities as other veterans did. However, he gradually realized that "witchery" was the constructed discourses to control people, and the decolonization of it finally rescued him from the trap of pre-given identity. So when diasporas had a keen insight on the mechanism of colonial discourse, there was a chance for them not to be manipulated by the colonial discourse that was decolonization or demystification. Thus, the postcolonial authoritative discourses were subversive and decentralized, and cultures were no longer considered as inherent, but constructed by the authority to maintain the hierarchical order as politics. When diasporas become unbound from the psychologically colonizing discourses and no longer perform the enforced identity, what should they perform and where should they gain their power?

When Tayo was unfettered by the colonial discourse or enforced identity, he then turned to gain power from nature or the organic wholeness of the ecosystem because cultural context could not provide him with the possibility to realize the self-identification. Only by breaking the cultural discourse and gaining power from other context, could diasporas negotiate freely in postcolonial situation. Then the protagonist found balance and strength in the process of exploring nature and got cured through Self-realization and negotiating with nature. He recognized himself from the interrelations of every existing element in nature and reached the ultimate recovery when it came to the realization of ecological holism. Tayo's recovery is the process of a combination of both decolonization of colonial discourses and Self-realization in nature.

The idea of Deep Ecology here suggested a harmonious lifestyle with nature and interdependent relationship with ecosystem. The realization of ecological self can be secured through the realization of the organic wholeness. That was where diasporas gained their power from other than cultural context. Nature was the source of strength for them to recover and reconstruct their diasporic identity. The diaspora experience of Tayo proved to be a positive example of identifying oneself through the interaction with natural elements. However, his recovery depending on the condition of specific diasporic category and unique Laguna tradition could not cover all the diasporas and stand for every single subject. So, the author claimed that the solution of nature context discussed in this book might have limitations. Also, there might be other contexts in addition to culture when considering other types of diasporas and it needed further research in the future.

All in all, it came to a conclusion for the problem of diaspora and diaspora identity that identity was just a criteria for categorizing diasporas but never the solution for diaspora situation. The author argued that a successful diaspora experience was the process of individual deconstruction of certain discourse and reconstruction of self, which required two elements, namely deconstruction and Self-realization. Deconstruction helped to get rid of the pre-given identity and free them from repetitive performances. It was important for diasporic subjects to figure out that it was the performativity that made them become diasporas, not the violently enforced identity. Due to the unprivileged cultural status, there was no way for diasporic groups to construct their identity in cultural context. So gaining power from other context rather than culture might provide possibilities for diasporas to realize and reconstruct themselves which is unfettered by the colonial discourses.

Appendix Ⅰ

Long time ago
in the beginning
there were no white people in this world
there was nothing European.
And this world might have gone on like that
except for one thing:
witchery.
This world was already complete
even without white people.
There was everything
including witchery.

Then it happened.
These witch people got together.

Some came from far far away
across oceans
across mountains.
Some had slanty eyes
others had black skin.
They all got together for a contest
the way people have baseball tournaments nowadays
except this was a contest
in dark things.

So anyway
they all got together
witch people from all directions
witches from all the Pueblos
and all the tribes.
They had Navajo witches there,
some from Hopi, and a few from Zuni.
They were having a witches' conference,
that's what it was
Way up in the lava rock hills
north of Cañoncito
they got together

to fool around in caves
with their animal skins.
Fox, badger, bobcat, and wolf
they circled the fire
and on the fourth time
they jumped into that animal's skin.

But this time it wasn't enough
and one of them
maybe a Sioux or some Eskimos
started showing off.
"That wasn't anything,
watch this."

The contest started like that.
Then some of them lifted the lids
on their big cooking pots,
calling the rest of them over
to take a look:
dead babies simmering in blood
circles of skull cut away
all the brains sucked out.

Witch medicine
to dry and grind into powder
for new victims.

Others untied skin bundles of disgusting objects:
dark flints, cinders from burned hogans where the dead lay
Whorls of skin
cut from fingertips
...

Finally there was only one
who hadn't shown off charms or powers.
The witch stood in the shadows beyond the fire
and no one ever knew where this witch came from
which tribe
or if it was a woman or a man.
But the important thing was
this witch didn't show off any dark thunder charcoals
or red ant-hill beads.
This one just told them to listen:
"What I have is a story."

At first they all laughed
but this witch said
Okay
go ahead
laugh if you want to
but as I tell the story
it will begin to happen.

Set in motion now
set in motion by our witchery
to work for us.

Caves across the ocean
in caves of dark hills
white skin people
like the belly of a fish
covered with hair.

Then they grow away from the earth
then they grow away from the sun
then they grow away from the plants and animals.
They see no life

When they look
they see only objects.
The world is a dead thing for them
the trees and rivers are not alive
the mountains and stones are not alive.
The deer and bear are objects
They see no life.

They fear
They fear the world.
They destroy what they fear.
They fear themselves.
The wind will blow them across the ocean
thousands of them in giant boats
swarming like larva
out of a crushed ant hill.

They will carry objects
which can shoot death
faster than the eye can see.

They will kill the things they fear

all the animals
the people will starve.

They will poison the water
they will spin the water away
and there will be drought
the people will starve.

They will fear what they find
They will fear the people
They kill what they fear.

Entire villages will be wiped out
They will slaughter whole tribes.

Corpses for us
Blood for us
Killing killing killing killing.

And those they do not kill
will die anyway
at the destruction they see

at the loss at the loss

of the children

the loss will destroy the rest.

Stolen rivers and mountains

the stolen land will eat their hearts

and jerk their mouths from the Mother.

The people will starve.

They will bring terrible diseases

the people have never known.

Entire tribes will die out

covered with festered sores

shitting blood

vomiting blood.

Corpses for our work

Set in motion now

set in motion by our witchery

set in motion

to work for us.

They will take this world from ocean to ocean

they will turn on each other
they will destroy each other
Up here
in these hills
they will find the rocks,
rocks with veins of green and yellow and black.
They will lay the final pattern with these rocks
they will lay it across the world
and explode everything.

Set in motion now
set in motion
To destroy
To kill
Objects to work for us
objects to act for us
Performing the witchery
for suffering
for torment
for the still-born
the deformed
the sterile
the dead.

Whirling

Whirling

Whirling

Whirling

set into motion now

set into motion.

So the other witches said

"Okay you win; you take the prize,

but what you said just now —

it isn't so funny

It doesn't sound so good.

We are doing okay without it

we can get along without that kind of thing.

Take it back.

Call that story back."

But the witch just shook its head

at the others in their stinking animal skins, fur and feathers.

It's already turned loose.

It's already coming.

It can't be called back.(Silko, 1977, pp.132-138)

Appendix Ⅱ

Up North
around Reedleaf Town
there was this Ck'o'yo magician
they called Kaup'a'ta or the Gambler.

He was tall
and he had a handsome face
but he always wore spruce greens around his head, over his eyes.
He dressed in the finest white buckskins
his moccasins were perfectly sewn.
He had strings of sky blue turquoise
strings of red coral in his ears.
In all ways
the Gambler was very good to look at.

His house was high
in the peaks of the Zuni mountains
and he waited for people to wander
up to his place.
He kept the gambling sticks all stacked up
ready for them.

He walked and turned around for them
to show off his fancy clothes and expensive beads.
Then he told them he would gamble with them —
their clothes, their beads for his.
Most people wore their old clothes
when they went hunting in the mountains;
so they figured they didn't have much to lose.
Anyway, they might win all his fine things.
Not many could pass up his offer.

But the people didn't know.
They ate the blue cornmeal
he offered them.
They didn't know
he mixed human blood with it.
Visitors who ate it

didn't have a chance.
He got power over them that way,
and when they started gambling with him
they did not stop until they lost
everything they owned.
And when they were naked
and he had everything
he'd say

"I tell you what
since I'm so good and generous
I'll give you one last chance.
See that rawhide bag hanging
on the north wall over there?
If you can guess what is in that bag
I'll give you back all your clothes and beads
and everything I have here too —
these feather blankets
all these strings of coral beads
these fine white buckskin moccasins.
But if you don't guess right
you lose your life."

They were in his power.
They had lost everything.
It was their last chance.
So they usually said "okay"
but they never guessed
what was in the bag.

He hung them upside down in his storeroom,
side by side with the other victims.
He cut out their hearts
and let their blood run down
into the bins of blue cornmeal.

That is what the ck'o'yo Kaup'a'ta, Gambler did,
up there
in the Zuni mountains.
And one time
he even captured the stormclouds.
He won everything from them
but since they can't be killed,
all he could do
was lock them up
in four rooms of his house —

the clouds of the east in the east room
the clouds of the south in the south room
the clouds of the west in the west room
the clouds of the north in the north room.

The Sun is their father.
Every morning he wakes them up.
But one morning he went
first to the north top of the west mountain
then to the west top of the south mountain
and then to the south top of the east mountain;
and finally, it was on the east top of the north mountain
he realized they were gone.

For three years the stormclouds disappeared
while the Gambler held them prisoners.
The land was drying up
the people and animals were starving.
They are his children
so he went looking for them.
He took blue pollen and yellow pollen
he took tobacco and coral beads;
and he walked into the open country

below the mesas.
There, in a sandy place by a blue flower vine,
Spiderwoman was waiting for him.

"Grandson," she said.
"I hear your voice," he answered
"but where are you?"
"Down here, by your feet."
He looked down at the ground and saw a little hole.

"I brought you something, Grandma."
"Why thank you, Grandson,
I can always use these things," she said.

"The stormclouds are missing."
"That Ck'o'yo Kaup'a'ta the Gambler has them locked up,"
she told him.
"How will I get them back?"

"It won't be easy, Grandson,
but here,
take this medicine.
Blow it on the Gambler's black ducks

who guard his place.
Take him by surprise.
The next thing is:
don't eat anything he offers you.
Go ahead
gamble with him.
Let him think he has you too.
Then he will make you his offer —
your life for a chance to win everything:
even his life.
He will say
"What do I have hanging in that leather bag
on my east wall?"
You say "Maybe some shiny pebbles,"
then you pause a while and say "Let me think."
Then guess again,
say "Maybe some mosquitoes."
He'll begin to rub his flint blade and say
"This is your last chance."
But this time you will guess
"The Pleiades!"
He'll jump up and say "Heheya'! You are the first to guess."
Next he will point to a woven cotton bag

hanging on the south wall.
He will say
"What is it I have in there?"
You'll say
"Could it be some bumblebees?"
He'll laugh and say "No!"
"Maybe some butterflies, the small yellow kind."
"Maybe some tiny black ants," you'll say.
"No!" Kaup'a'ta will be smiling then.
"This is it," he'll say.

But this is the last time, Grandson,
you say "Maybe you have Orion in there."
And then
everything—
his clothing, his beads, his heart
and the rainclouds
will be yours."

"Okay, Grandma, I'll go."
He took the medicine into the Zuni mountains.
He left the trail and walked high on one of the peaks.
The black ducks rushed at him

but he blew the medicine on them
before they could squawk.

He came up behind the Gambler
practicing with the sticks
on the floor of his house.

"I'm fasting," he told Kaup'a'ta,
when he offered him the blue cornmeal
"but thanks anyway."
Sun Man pulled out his things:
four sets of new clothes
two pairs of new moccasins
two strings of white shell beads
Kaup'a'ta smiled when he saw these things
"We'll gamble all night," he said.

It happened
just the way Spiderwoman said:
When he had lost everything
Kaup'a'ta gave him a last chance.
The Gambler bet everything he had
that Sun Man couldn't guess what he had

in the bag on the east wall.
Kaup'a'ta was betting his life
that he couldn't guess
what was in the sack hanging from the south wall.

"Heheya'! You guessed right!
Take this black flint knife, Sun Man,
go ahead, cut out my heart, kill me."
Kaup'a'ta lay down on the floor
with his head toward the east.
But Sun Man knew Kaup'a'ta was magical
and he couldn't be killed anyway.
Kaup'a'ta was going to lie there
and pretend to be dead.
So Sun Man knew what to do:
He took the flint blade
and he cut out the Gambler's eyes
He threw them into the south sky
and they became the horizon stars of autumn.

Then he opened the doors of the four rooms
and he called to the stormclouds:
"My children," he said

I have found you!

Come on out. Come home again.

Your mother, the earth is crying for you.

Come home, children, come home."(Silko, 1977, pp.170-176)

Bibliography

Anderson, B. (1991). *Imagined communities: Reflections on the origin and spread of nationalism*. London: Verso.

Anthias, F. (1998). Evaluating "diaspora": Beyond ethnicity. *Sociology*, 32(3), 557-580.

Anwar, M. (1998). *Between cultures: Continuity and change in the lives of young Asians*. London: Routledge.

Appadurai, A. (1996). *Modernity at large: Cultural dimensions of globalization*. Minneapolis: University of Minnesota Press.

Assmann, J., & Czaplicka, J. (1995). Collective memory and cultural identity. *New German Critique*, 65, 125-133.

Barkan, E., & Shelton, M. D. (1998). *Borders, exiles, diasporas*. Stanford: Stanford University Press.

Barthes, R. (2009). *Mythologies*. New York: Vintage.

Behdad, A. (1997). Nationalism and immigration to the United States. *Diaspora: A Journal of Transnational Studies*, 6(2), 155-178.

Bhabha, H. K. (1985). Signs taken for wonders: Questions of ambivalence and authority under a tree outside Delhi, May 1817. *Critical Inquiry*, 12(1), 144-165.

Bhabha, H. K. (1990). The third space: Interview with Homi Bhabha. In J. Rutherford (Ed.), *Community, culture, difference*. London: Lawrence and Wishart.

Bhabha, H.K. (1994). *The location of culture*. New York: Routledge.

Bhabha, H.K. (1996). Culture's in-between. *Questions of Cultural Identity*, (1), 53-60.

Bhabha, H. K. (2009). In the cave of making: Thoughts on third space. In K. Ikas, & G. Wagner (Eds.), *Communicating in the third space*. New York: Routledge.

Bhabha, H. K. (2013). The other question: difference, discrimination and the discourse of colonialism. In F. Barker, P. Hulme, M. Iversen, & D. Loxley (Eds.), *Literature politics & theory*. New York: Routledge.

Bhabha, H. K. (2015). "The beginning of their real enunciation": Stuart Hall and the work of culture. *Critical Inquiry*, 42(1), 1-30.

Bird, G. (2005). Towards a decolonization of the mind and text: Leslie Marmon Silko's *Ceremony*. In I. Hernández-Avila(Ed.), *Reading Native American women: Critical / creative representations*. Altamira Press.

Bolt, P. J. (1996). Looking to the diaspora: The overseas Chinese and China's economic development, 1978-1994. *Diaspora: A Journal of Transnational Studies*, 5(3), 467-496.

Brah, A. (1996). *Cartographies of diaspora: Contesting identities*. New York: Routledge.

Braziel, J. E., & Mannur, A. (Eds.) (2003). *Theorizing diaspora: A reader*. Malden, MA: Blackwell.

Brubaker, R., & Cooper, F. (2000). Beyond "identity". *Theory and Society*, 29(1), 1-47.

Burke, E. (1976). Frantz Fanon's "The Wretched of the Earth". *Daedalus*, 105(1), 127-135.

Butler, J. (2006). *Gender trouble*. New York: Routledge.

Butler, J. (2011). *Bodies that matter: On the discursive limits of sex*. New York: Routledge.

Butler, J. (2013). Contingent foundations: Feminism and the question of "postmodernism". In J. Butler & J. W. Scott (Eds.), *Feminists theorize the political*. New York: Routledge.

Butler, K. D. (2001). Defining diaspora, refining a

discourse. *Diaspora: A Journal of Transnational Studies*, 10(2), 189-219.

Castles, S., De Haas, H., & Miller, M. J. (2013). *The age of migration: International population movements in the modern world*. London: Macmillan International Higher Education.

Chatterjee, P. (1993). *Nationalist thought and the colonial world: A derivative discourse*. Minneapolis: University of Minnesota Press.

Cheah, P., Grosz, E., Butler, J., & Cornell, D. (1998). The future of sexual difference: An interview with Judith Butler and Drucilla Cornell. *Diacritics*, 28(1), 19-42.

Cheah, P. (1997). Given culture: Rethinking cosmopolitical freedom in transnationalism. *Boundary 2*, 24(2), 157-197.

Chernaik, L. (1996). Spatial displacements: Transnationalism and the new social movements. *Gender, Place and Culture: A Journal of Feminist Geography*, 3(3), 251-276.

Cheung, K. K. (Ed.) (1997). *An interethnic companion to Asian American literature*. Cambridge: Cambridge University Press.

Chow, R. (1993). *Writing diaspora: Tactics of intervention in contemporary cultural studies*. Bloomington: Indiana University Press.

Cipolla, C. (2017, January 10). Native American diaspora and ethnogenesis. *Oxford Handbooks Online*. Retrieved 23 Dec. 2019, from https://www.oxfordhandbooks.com/view/10.1093/oxfordhb/9780199935413. 001. 0001/oxfordhb-9780199935413-e-69.

Clarke, J., Hall, S., Jefferson, T., & Roberts, B. (2006). Subcultures, cultures and class. In S. Hall, &T. Jefferson (Eds.), *Resistance through rituals*. London: Routledge.

Clifford, J. (1988). *The Predicament of culture*. Cambridge: Harvard University Press.

Clifford, J. (1992). Travelling cultures. In L. Grossberg, C. Nelson, & P. Treichler (Eds.), *Cultural studies*. New York: Routledge.

Clifford, J. (1994). Diasporas. *Cultural Anthropology*, 9(3), 302-338.

Cohen, R. (1992). The diaspora of a diaspora: The case of the Caribbean. *Social Science Information*, 31(1), 159-169.

Cohen, R. (1996). Diasporas and the nation-state: From victims to challengers. *International Affairs*, 72(3), 507-520.

Cohen, R. (2008). *Global diasporas: An introduction*. London: Routledge.

Connor, W. (1986). The impact of homelands upon

diasporas. In G. Sheffer (Ed.), *Modern diasporas in international politics*. New York: St. Martin's Press.

Côté, J. E. (1996). Sociological perspectives on identity formation: The culture-identity link and identity capital. *Journal of Adolescence*, 19(5), 417-428.

Dayal, S. (1996a). Diaspora and double consciousness. *The Journal of the Midwest Modern Language Association*, 29(1), 46-62.

Dayal, S. (1996b). Postcolonialism's possibilities: Subcontinental diasporic intervention. *Cultural Critique*, 33, 113-149.

Derrida, J. (1982). Difference. In *Margins of philosophy*, trans. Bass, A. Chicago: University of Chicago Press.

Devall, B., & Sessions, G. (1985). *Deep ecology*. Layton: Gibbs Smith Publishers.

Dickstein, M. (1993). After the Cold War: Culture as politics, politics as culture. *Social Research*, 60(3), 531-544.

Donald, J., & Rattansi, A. (Eds.) (1992). "*Race*", *culture and difference*. New Delhi: Sage.

Drew, J. (1998). Cultural composition: Stuart Hall on ethnicity and the discursive turn. *JAC*, 18(2), 171-196.

Evasdaughter, E. N. (1988). Leslie Marmon Silko's *Ceremony*: Healing ethnic hatred by mixed-breed laughter.

Melus, 15(1), 83-95.

Fairchild, H. H. (1994). Frantz Fanon's *The wretched of the earth* in contemporary perspective. *Journal of Black Studies*, 25(2), 191-199.

Fanon, F. (1963). *The wretched of the earth*. New York: Grove Press.

Foucault, M. (1980). *Power / knowledge: Selected interviews and other writings, 1972-1977*. New York: Vintage.

Fraser, N. (1997). Heterosexism, misrecognition, and capitalism: A response to Judith Butler. *Social Text*, 52/53, 279-289.

Friedman, J. (1994). *Cultural identity and global process*. New Delhi: Sage.

Grossberg, L. (1986). History, politics and postmodernism: Stuart Hall and cultural studies. *Journal of Communication Inquiry*, 10(2), 61-77.

Gupta, A., & Ferguson, J. (1992). Beyond "culture": space, identity, and the politics of difference. *Cultural Anthropology*, 7(1), 6-23.

Habib, J. (2019). *Israel, diaspora, and the routes of national belonging*. Toronto: University of Toronto Press.

Hall, S. (1990). Cultural identity and diaspora. In J.

Rutherford (Ed.), *Identity: Community, culture, difference*. London: Lawrence & Wishart.

Hall, S. (1991a). Ethnicity, identity and difference. *Radical America*, 23(4), 9-20.

Hall, S. (1991b). The local and the global: Globalization and ethnicity. In D. K. Anthony (Ed.), *Culture, globalization and world-system: Contemporary condition for the representation of identity*. Basingstoke: Macmillan.

Hall, S. (1992a). New Ethnicities. In J. Donald, & A. Rattansi (Eds.), '*Race*', *culture & difference*. New Delhi: Sage.

Hall, S. (1992b). Race, culture, and communications: Looking backward and forward at cultural studies. *Rethinking Marxism*, 5(1), 10-18.

Hall, S., & Du Gay, P. (Eds.) (1996). *Questions of cultural identity*. New Delhi: Sage.

Hall, G., & Wortham, S. (1997). Rethinking authority: Interview with Homi K. Bhabha. *Angelaki*, 2(2), 59-63.

Hall, S., Evans, J., & Nixon, S. (2013). *Representation*. New Delhi: Sage.

Hear, N. V. (1998). *New diasporas: The mass exodus, dispersal and regrouping of migrant communities*. London: UCL Press.

Hermans, H. J., & Dimaggio, G. (2007). Self, identity, and globalization in times of uncertainty: A dialogical analysis. *Review of General Psychology*, 11(1), 31-61.

Hobbs, M. (1994). Living in-between: Tayo as radical reader in Leslie Marmon Silko's *Ceremony*. *Western American Literature*, 28(4), 301-312.

Hussain, Y. (2017). *Writing diaspora: South Asian women, culture and ethnicity*. London: Routledge.

Innes, C. L. (2007). *The Cambridge introduction to postcolonial literatures in English*. Cambridge: Cambridge University Press.

Jahner, E. (1979). An act of attention: Event structure in "Ceremony". *American Indian Quarterly*, 5(1), 37-46.

Jameson, F. (1991). *Postmodernism and the cultural logic of late capitalism*. London: Verso.

JanMohamed, A. (1995). Refiguring values, power, knowledge, or Foucault's disavowal of Marx. In B. Magnus, & S. Cullenberg (Eds.), *Whither Marxism?: Global crises in international perspective*. New York and London: Routledge.

Jinadu, L. A. (1978). Some African theorists of culture and modernization: Fanon, Cabral and some others. *African Studies Review*, 21(1), 121-138.

Kenny, K. (2013). *Diaspora: A very short introduction*.

New York: Oxford University Press.

King, A. D. (Ed.) (1991). *Culture, globalization and the world system: Contemporary conditions for the representation of identity* (Vol. 3). Minneapolis: University of Minnesota Press.

Koshy, S. (1996). The fiction of Asian American literature. *The Yale Journal of Criticism*, 9(2), 315-346.

Kroeber, A. L., & Kluckhohn, C. (1952). *Culture: A critical review of concepts and definitions*. Cambridge, Massachusetts: Harvard University Press.

Kuortti, J., & Nyman, J. (Eds.) (2007). *Reconstructing hybridity: Post-colonial studies in transition*. Amsterdam: Rodopi.

Lavie, S., & Swedenburg, T. (1996). *Displacement, diaspora, and geographies of identity*. Durham: Duke University Press.

Lim, S. L. (1993). Feminist and ethnic literary theories in Asian American literature. *Feminist Studies*, 19(3), 571-595.

Lim, S., & Ling, A. (Eds.). (1992). *Reading the literatures of Asian America*. Philadelphia: Temple University Press.

Lowe, L. (1991). Heterogeneity, hybridity, multiplicity: Marking Asian American differences. *Asian American Studies*, (1), 254.

Lowe, L. (1996). *Immigrant acts: On Asian American cultural politics*. Durham, NC: Duke University Press.

Lowe, L. (1998). Work, immigration, gender: New subjects of cultural politics. *Social Justice*, 73(3), 31-49.

Ma, S. (1998). *Immigrant subjectivities in Asian American and Asian diaspora literatures*. Albany: State University of New York Press.

Mazrui, A.A. (1990). *Cultural forces in world politics*. London: James Currey.

Moore-Gilbert, B. (1997). *Postcolonial theory: Context, practices, politics*. London and New York: Verso.

Naess, A. (1973). The shallow and the deep, long-range ecology movement: A summary. *Inquiry*, 16(1-4), 95-100.

Naess, A. (1990). *Ecology, community and lifestyle: Outline of an ecosophy*. Cambridge: Cambridge University Press.

Naess, A. (1995). The deep ecological movements. In G. Sessions (Ed.), Deep ecology for the 21century. Boston and London: Shambhala Press.

Nursey-Bray, P. (1980). Race and nation: Ideology in the thought of Frantz Fanon. *The Journal of Modern African Studies*, 18(1), 135-142.

Oakes, L. (2001). *Language and national identity: Comparing France and Sweden*. Amsterdam: John Benjamins Publishing.

Parry, B. (1994). Signs of our times: Discussion of Homi Bhabha's *The location of culture*. *Third Text*, 28-29 (8), 5-24.

Peck, J. (2001). Itinerary of a thought: Stuart Hall, cultural studies, and the unresolved problem of the relation of culture to "not culture". *Cultural Critique*, 48, 200-249.

Prasad, M. M. (2014). Emergence: Stuart Hall and cultural studies across the world. *Inter-Asia Cultural Studies*, 15(2), 191-193.

Rice, D. A. (2005). Witchery, indigenous resistance, and urban space in Leslie Marmon Silko's *Ceremony*. *Studies in American Indian Literatures*, 17(4), 114-143.

Ricoeur, P. (1994). *Oneself as another*. Chicago: University of Chicago Press.

Rose, G. (1995). The interstitial perspective: A review essay on Homi Bhabha's *The location of culture*. *Environment and Planning D: Society and Space*, 13(3), 365-373.

Ruppert, J. (1993). Dialogism and Mediation in Leslie Silko's *Ceremony*. *The Explicator*, 51(2), 129-134.

Said, E. (1978). *Orientalism*. New York: Pantheon

Books.

Said, E. (1993). *Culture and imperialism*. New York: Alfred A. Knopf.

Safran, W. (1991). Diasporas in modern societies: Myths of homeland and return. *Diaspora: A Journal of Transnational Studies*, 1(1), 83-99.

Salleh, A. K. (1984). Deeper than deep ecology: The eco-feminist connection. *Environmental Ethics*, 6(4), 339-345.

San Juan, E. (2019). *From exile to diaspora: Versions of the Filipino experience in the United States*. New York: Routledge.

Sessions, G. (1987). The deep ecology movement: A review. *Environmental Review*, 11(2), 105-125.

Sheffer, G. (2003). *Diaspora politics: At home and abroad*. Cambridge: Cambridge University Press.

Silko, L. M. (1986). *Ceremony*. New York: Penguin.

Silko, L. M. (1977). *Ceremony*. New York: Penguin.

Smith, A. D. (1991). *National identity*. Harmondsworth: Penguin.

Spivak, G. C. (1987). *In other world: Essays in cultural politics*. London: Methuen.

Spivak, G. C. (1994). Can the subaltern speak? In P. Williams & L. Chrisman (Eds.), *Colonial discourse and postcolonial theory*. New York: Columbia University Press.

Spivak, G. C. (1999). *A critique of postcolonial reason*. Cambridge: Harvard University Press.

Stein, R. (2002). Contested ground: Nature, narrative, and Native American identity in Leslie Marmon Silko's *Ceremony*. In A. R. Chavkin (Ed.), *Leslie Marmon Silko's Ceremony: A Casebook* (pp. 193-211). New York: Oxford University Press.

Stephens, M. A. (1998). Black transnationalism and the politics of national identity: West Indian intellectuals in Harlem in the age of war and revolution. *American Quarterly*, 50(3), 592-608.

Steven V., & Cohen R. (Eds.) (1999). *Migration, diaspora and transnationalism*. Cheltenham: Edward Elgar.

Suh, E. M. (2002). Culture, identity consistency, and subjective well-being. *Journal of Personality and Social Psychology*, 83(6), 1378.

Tölölyan, K. (1994). Diasporama. *Diaspora: A Journal of Transnational Studies*, 3(2), 235-235.

Tölölyan, K. (1996). Rethinking diaspora(s): Stateless power in the transnational moment. *Diaspora: A Journal of Transnational Studies*, 5(1), 3-36.

Tölölyan, K. (2000). Elites and institutions in the

Armenian transnation. *Diaspora: A Journal of Transnational Studies*, 9(1), 107-136.

Tuck, E., & Yang, K. W. (2012). Decolonization is not a metaphor. *Decolonization: Indigeneity, Education & Society*, 1 (1), 1-40.

Van Hear, N. (1998). New diasporas: The mass exodus, dispersal and regrouping of migrant communities. *New Diasporas*. London: ULC Press.

Vergès, F. (1997). Creole skin, black mask: Fanon and disavowal. *Critical Inquiry*, 23(3), 578-595.

Voicu, C. G. (2013). Cultural identity and diaspora. *Philobiblon: Transylvanian Journal of Multidisciplinary Research in Humanities*, 18(1), 161-174.

Wallerstein, I. (2009). Reading Fanon in the 21st century. *New Left Review*, 57, 117-125.

West, C. (1990). The new cultural politics of difference. *October*, 53, 93-109.

Wong, S. L. C. (1993). *Reading Asian American literature: From necessity to extravagance*. Princeton: Princeton University Press.

Wood, B. (1998). Stuart Hall's cultural studies and the problem of hegemony. *British Journal of Sociology*, 49(3), 399-414.

Acknowledgements

This book is published on the basis of my doctoral dissertation. I started to focus on this topic in the first year of my doctoral curriculum when I was studying with my adviser on the related issues of ethnic American literature. Most of the chapters were written during that time. My first and deepest thanks go to my adviser Professor Lee, Suk Hee, who enlightened me on the subject of diaspora and inspired me throughout the whole process of studying and writing. She carefully commented and suggested on each and every section of the manuscript to keep me on track. It was her support and encouragement on every stage of my work that made me go through all the difficulties. Thanks also go to Professor Jung, Hyun Kyoung, Professor Kwack, Dong Gi, Professor Park, Min Sun who gave me lectures over the academic years. Besides the prescribed courses, they as well gave me insightful suggestions that broadened my vision. I learnt a lot from them.

My deep appreciation goes to editors at Shandong University Press, for their expertly steering this project through and meticulously proofreading to save me from embarrassing mistakes. It was their help and support that made this book possible.

My gratitude, finally, goes to my family members for their selfless dedication. My husband was always there comforting and encouraging me when I felt confused and got stuck. My parents, standing behind all the time, gave me enormous power and determination to achieve the task. My son, the lovely little kid, was so well-behaved and quiet during my study. I love them all.